"He was on an island that seemed to be part of Lone, Majesty," I said. "He—er—sort of followed us."

"Or followed you," the Queen said. She turned to Aunt Beck again. "You are very lucky to have such a gifted assistant," she said.

I knew I was blushing redder than Ogo. Aunt Beck shot me a scathing look and answered in her driest way, "If gifted means secretly adopting a stray cat, then I suppose I am lucky, yes."

This did not please the Queen at all. Her beautiful eyes narrowed, and she said, quite fiercely, "I know this cat. He would only follow someone of great abilities."

Aunt Beck shrugged, "I've no idea what Aileen's abilities might be."

⤻

"Jones's imaginative vigor is unabated in this last, picaresque novel; her deft, fluid style and penchant for precise, characterful description are amply present in Aileen's voice as she recounts her journey." —*The Horn Book*

DIANA WYNNE JONES

THE ISLANDS OF CHALDEA

Completed by Ursula Jones

Greenwillow Books

An Imprint of HarperCollinsPublishers

The Islands of Chaldea
Copyright © 2014 by the Estate of Diana Wynne Jones and Ursula Jones
First published in 2014 in in hardcover, first Greenwillow paperback 2015.

www.harpercollinschildrens.com

The right of Ursula Jones to be identified as the co-author of this work has been asserted by her.

The text of this book is set in Electra LH.
Book design by Sylvie Le Floc'h
Map by Sally Taylor

Library of Congress Cataloging-in-Publication Data

Jones, Diana Wynne.
The islands of Chaldea / by Diana Wynne Jones ; completed by Ursula Jones.
pages cm
"Greenwillow Books."
Summary: Aileen's family of magic makers includes Aunt Beck, the most powerful magician on Skarr, but her own magic does not show itself until a mission for the King and a magical cat help her find strength and confidence.
ISBN 978-0-06-229507-1 (trade ed.)—ISBN 978-0-06-229508-8 (pbk.)
[1. Magic—Fiction. 2. Aunts—Fiction. 3. Self-confidence—Fiction. 4. Cats—Fiction.
5. Voyages and travels—Fiction.] I. Jones, Ursula. II. Title.
PZ7.J684Isl 2013 [Fic]—dc23 2013036422

15 16 17 18 19 CG/RRDH 10 9 8 7 6 5 4 3 2 1
First Edition

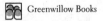 Greenwillow Books

THE ISLANDS OF
CHALDEA

A map to indicate
THE ISLANDS OF CHALDEA
and neighboring Logra

ᦙ I ᦙ

Porridge is my Aunt Beck's answer to everything.

The morning after my initiation proved to be such a complete failure she gave me porridge with cream and honey—an unheard-of luxury in our little stone house—and I was almost too upset to enjoy it. I sat shivering and my teeth chattered, as much with misery as with cold, and pushed the stuff about with my spoon, until Aunt Beck wrapped me in a big fluffy plaid and told me sharply that it was not the end of the world.

"Or not yet," she added. "And your pigtail is almost in the honey."

This made me sit up a little. Yesterday I had washed my hair in cold springwater full of herbs—washed all over in it as well—and it was not an experience I wanted to repeat. I had gone without food too all day before that dreadful washing, with the result that I felt damp and chilly all over, and tender as a snail's horns, when the time came for me to go down into the Place. And I hadn't got any drier or warmer as the night went on.

The Place, you see, is like a deep trench in the ground lined with slabs of stone, with more stone slabs atop of it covered with turf. You slide down a leafy ramp to get into it, and Aunt Beck pulls another stone slab across the entrance to shut you in. Then you sit there in nothing but a linen petticoat waiting for something to happen—or, failing that, for morning. There is nothing to smell but stone and damp and distant turf, nothing to feel but cold—particularly underneath you as you sit—and nothing to see but darkness.

You are supposed to have visions, or at least to be

visited by your guardian animal. All the women of my family have gone down into the Place when they were twelve years old and the moon was right, and most of them seem to have had the most interesting time. My mother saw a line of princes walking slowly past her, all silvery and pale and crowned with gold circlets. I remember her telling me before she died. Aunt Beck seems to have seen a whole menagerie of animals — all the lithe kinds like snakes, lizards, greyhounds, and running deer, which strikes me as typical — and in addition, she says, all the charms and lore she had ever learned fell into place in her head, into a marvelous sensible pattern. She has been a tremendously powerful magicmaker ever since.

Nothing like that happened to me. Nothing happened at all.

No, I tell a lie. I messed it up. And I didn't dare tell Aunt Beck. I sat there and I sat there with my arms wrapped around my knees, trying to keep warm and trying not to notice the numb cold seeping up from the hard corners of my bones that I was sitting on and trying, above all, not to be scared silly about what was going to happen. The worst and most frightening thing was being shut in underground. I didn't dare move because I was sure I would find that the side walls had moved inward and the stone roof had moved down. I just sat, shivering. A lot of the time I had my eyes squeezed shut, but some of the time I forced myself to open my eyes. I was afraid that the visions would come and I wouldn't see them because my eyes were shut.

And you know how your eyes play tricks in the dark. After a long, long time, probably at least one eternity, I thought that there was a light coming into the Place from somewhere. And I thought, Bless my soul, it's morning! Aunt Beck must have overslept and forgotten to come and let me out at dawn! This was because I seemed to have sat there for such hours that I was positive it must be nearly lunchtime by then. So I scrambled myself around in the faint light, scraping one elbow and bumping both knees, until I was facing the ramp. The faint light did, honestly, seem to be coming in round the edges of the stone slab Aunt Beck had heaved across at the top.

That was enough to put me into a true panic. I raced up that leafy slope on my hands and knees and tried to draw the slab aside. When it wouldn't budge, I screamed at it to *open and let me out! At once!* And I heaved at it like a mad thing.

Rather to my surprise it slid across quite easily then and I shot out of the Place like a rabbit. There I reared up on my knees more astonished than ever. It was bright moonlight. The full moon was riding high and small and almost golden, casting frosty whiteness on every clump of heather and every rock and making a silver cube of our small house just down the hill. I could see the mountains for miles in one direction and in the other the silver-dark line of the sea. It was so moon-quiet that I could actually *hear* the sea. It was making that small secret sound you hear inside a seashell. And it was as cold out there as if the whiteness on the heather was really the frost it looked like.

I gave a great shudder of cold and shame as I looked up at the moon again. From the height of it I could see it was the middle of the night still. I had only been inside the Place for three hours at the most. And I couldn't possibly have seen the moon from inside. It was in the wrong part of the sky.

At this it came to me that the pale light I'd seen in there had really been the start of a vision. I had made an awful mistake and interrupted it. The idea so frightened me that I plunged back down inside and seized the stone slab and heaved mightily and pulled it across the opening anyhow, before I slid right back down to the stone floor and crouched there desperately.

"Oh, please come back!" I said to the vision. "I'll be good. I won't move an inch now."

But nothing else happened. It seemed quite dark in

the Place and much warmer now, out of the wind, but though I crouched there for hours with my eyes wide open, I never saw another thing.

In the dawn, when I heard Aunt Beck drawing back the slab, I gave a great start of terror, because I was sure she would notice that the stone had been moved. But it was still half dark, and I suppose it was the last thing she expected. Anyway she did not seem to see anything unusual. Besides, she says I was fast asleep. She had to slide down beside me and shake my shoulder. But I heard her do that. I feel so deceitful. And such a failure.

"Well, Aileen," she said as she helped me up the ramp—I was very stiff by then—"what happened to you?"

"Nothing!" I wailed, and I burst into tears.

Aunt Beck always gets quite brisk when people cry. She hates having to show sympathy. She put a coat around me and marched me away downhill, saying, "Stop that noise now, Aileen. There's nothing to be ashamed of in that. Maybe it's too soon for you. It happens. My grandmother—your great-grandmother Venna, that is—had to go down into the Place three times before she saw anything, and then it was only a wee scrap of a hedgehog."

"But maybe I'm no good," I blubbered. "Maybe the magic's diluted in me because my father was a foreigner."

"What blather," said Aunt Beck. "Your father was a bard from Gallis, and your mother chose him with great care. 'Beck,' she said to me, 'this man has the true gift, and I am determined to have a child from him with gifts even greater.' Mind you, after he went the way of Prince Alasdair, this didn't prevent her losing her head over the Priest of Kilcannon."

And dying of it, I thought miserably. My mother died trying to bring a brother for me into the world. The baby died too, and Aunt Beck, who is my mother's younger sister, has had to bring me up since I was five years old.

"But never fear," Aunt Beck went on. "I have

noted all along that you have the makings of a great magicworker. It will come. We'll just have to try again at the next full moon."

Saying which, she led me indoors to the sound of the cow mooing and the hens clucking in the next room and sat me down in front of the porridge. I think much of my misery, as I sat and pushed rivers of cream into pools of honey, was at the thought of having to go through all that again.

"Eat it!" snapped Aunt Beck.

So I did, and it made me feel somewhat better— better enough anyway to trudge to my narrow little bed and fall asleep there until the sun had turned back down the sky in the early afternoon. I might have slept even longer, except that someone came knocking at Aunt Beck's door.

"Open!" he said pompously. "Open in the name of the King!"

It turned out to be the Logran boy, very proud of the way his voice had broken all deep and manly. Only last week he was squeaking and roaring all over the place and people were laughing at him even more than usual. Aunt Beck opened the door, and he came striding in, looking quite grand in a new uniform with the heavy pleats of the King's plaid swinging over one shoulder. People up at the castle may despise him and call him the Ogre from Logra, but I will say this for my distant cousin the King: he keeps the boy well provided for. He is always well dressed and is as well educated as I am—and I go up to the castle for lessons three days a week—and I think they train him in arms too. Anyway, he had a fine sword belted across his skinny hips over the combed-out sheepskin of his new jacket. I suspect he was prouder of that sword than he was even of his big new voice.

He came marching in in all his splendor and then stopped dead, staring and stammering. He had never been in our house before. First he was obviously dismayed at how small the room was, with me propped up on one elbow in bed just beyond the cooking fire, and then he was astonished at Aunt Beck's paintings. Aunt Beck is quite an artist. She says it is the chief gift of us people of Skarr. Our room is surrounded in paintings—there are portraits of me, of my poor dead mother, and of any shepherd or fisherman who is rash enough to agree to sit still for her. My favorite is a lovely group of the castle children gathered, squabbling and giggling, on the steps up to the hall with the light all slantways over them in golden zigzags up the steps. But there are landscapes too—mountains, moors, and sea—and several paintings of boats. Aunt Beck has even painted the screen that hides her bed to look like one of the walls, with shelves of jars and vials and a string of onions on it.

This boy—his name is a strange Logran one that sounds like Ogo, which accounts for his nickname— stared at all of it with his big smooth head thrust forward and his white, spotty face wrinkled in astonishment. He had to stare hard at the screen before he could decide that this was a painting too. His ugly face flushed all pink then because he thought it was a real wall at first.

"What's the matter, Ogo?" said Aunt Beck. Like everyone else, she is a bit sarcastic with him.

"Th-these," he stammered. "This is all so beautiful, so real. And"—he pointed to the group of children on the steps—"I am in this one."

He was too, though I had never realized it before. He was the smallest one, being shoved off the bottom step by a bigger boy, who was probably my cousin Ivar. Aunt Beck is very clever. She had done them all from quick charcoal sketches, and none of them had ever known they were being painted.

A smug, gratified expression gathered in the creases of Aunt Beck's lean face. She is not immune to praise, but she likes everyone to think she is strict and passionless. "Don't forget to give your message," she said. "What was it?"

"Oh, yes." Ogo stood to attention, with his head almost brushing the beams. He had grown a lot recently and was even taller than Aunt Beck. "I am to fetch both of you to the castle for dinner," he said. "The King wishes to consult with you."

"In that case," said Aunt Beck, "will you take a mug of my beer and sit outside while Aileen gets herself dressed?"

Ogo shot a flustered look somewhere in the direction of the shelves over my head. He was very embarrassed at seeing me in bed wearing next to nothing and had been avoiding looking anywhere near me up to then. "If she's ill," he blustered, "she ought not to come."

"You're very considerate," said Aunt Beck, "but she's not ill—just a little tired—and we'll both be ready directly. Outside with you now." And she clapped a mug into his large pink hands and steered him out of the door again to the bench that catches the sun and the view of the sea. "Hurry up," she said to me as she clapped the door shut behind him. "The blue dress and the best plaid, and don't forget to wash first. I'll do your hair when you're ready."

I got up with a groan as Aunt Beck vanished behind

the painted screen. I was stiff all over and still inclined to shiver. And Aunt Beck is so fussy about washing. I felt I had washed half to death yesterday, and here she was expecting me to get wet all over again. But I didn't dare disobey. I knew from bitter experience that she could always tell when I'd only wet the bowl and the face flannel. She never said she knew, but the hair combing that followed was always punishing.

I dressed gloomily, wondering what King Kenig wanted now. He consults Aunt Beck once a week anyway, but he seldom bothers to include me. In fact, there's quite a battle there because Aunt Beck nearly always takes me along as part of my education. Then my distant cousin King Kenig scowls and rakes at his beard and snarls something about not needing the infantry, and Aunt Beck just gives him one of her diamond-hard smiles, very sweetly, and I usually have to stay, listening to the King asking about the omens for a raid on his neighbors or what to do about the crops this year. The only interesting times are when Aunt Beck calls for the silver bowl to be filled and does a scrying for him. I like to watch that—not that I can ever see anything in the bowl, but I like to watch my aunt seeing. It gives you an exciting sort of shiver up your back when she says in a strange, groaning voice, "I see fires up on the Peak of Storms and cattle stampeding." She's always right too. When she said that, the clans of Cormack raided from the next kingship, but thanks to Aunt Beck, our people were ready for them. I even got to see a bit of the fighting.

Anyway, as you will have gathered from this, Aunt Beck is a Wise Woman as well as a magicworker, as all the women of our family are. The men born to us marry outside the family. This is how King Kenig comes to be a distant cousin. My great-great-grandmother's brother married the sister of the then King, and their son was King Kenig's grandfather. At one time our family was a large one, reputed to have the best Wise Women on the entire huge island of Skarr, but that was in the time of the Twelve Sisters of Kenneal. Now Aunt Beck and

I are the only ones left. But Aunt Beck is still said to be the best there is.

She looked the part too when she came out from behind the screen in her best dress and set about combing out my hair. My hair was still damp, and there was a lot of tugging to get the stray bits of herb out of it.

～II～

It is a couple of miles to the castle, over the moor and down to the foreland, but it seemed longer because a mist came down and hid all the distances. I was tired. I trudged through the heather behind the other two, feeling small and untidy and a failure. Some of the time I was trying not to cry at the idea of having to spend another night in the Place in a month's time.

Even if I did get initiated, then I knew with a dreadful certainty that I would never, ever be the equal of Aunt Beck. Oh, I had memorized the cantrips and procedures all right, and I knew all my herbs and weather lore, but it takes more than that to be a proper magicwoman. I had only to look at my aunt's tall, narrow figure striding elegantly ahead, with her plaid stylishly not quite wrapping her small, dark, neatly plaited head, to know that. Aunt Beck's best boots had red cork heels—they cost the earth because they came from Logra before the blockade—and never once did a splash of mud or spray of heather cling to those gleaming scarlet cubes. My feet were muddy all over already. My hair is a messy pale brown, and *nothing* seems to stop wisps of it separating from my pigtails. They flapped beside my face, fuzzy already. And I am short for my age. Even the younger children in the castle were taller than me now, and I couldn't see myself ever being tall or wise. I shall always be that little Aileen with the freckles and the buckteeth and no real gift at all, I thought sadly. Damn it, even *Ogo* looked more imposing than me.

Ogo had new shoes that laced up over his smart new trews to his knees. They must have taken a deal of leather to make because Ogo's feet are *enormous*. They looked even bigger on the ends of his skinny, laced-up legs. I could see he was treading very carefully not to spoil them in the peat. I guessed he had promised the shoemaker to keep that pair good at least.

Poor Ogo. Everyone at the castle scolded him or jeered. He is a foreigner and different from the rest. As far as I knew, he had been left behind ten years ago, when the magicmen of Logra cast the spells that made it impossible for anyone from Skarr—or Bernica, or Gallis, for that matter—to cross the sea to Logra. Logra might be on the moon now for all that we can do to get to it.

We were at war with Logra then. We always are. All the same, there were quite a few families of Lograns on Skarr, traders and ambassadors and priests and so forth, who all fled to boats on the night of the spell casting. One or two others got left behind as well as Ogo—the mad old spinning woman up in Kilcannon for one, and the man who claimed to be a scholar whom the Cormacks arrested as a spy—but Ogo was the only child.

I believe he was five at the time. I suppose his relatives were traders or something who fled with the rest and simply forgot him. I think the worse of them for that. According to Ogo, some of them were magicmen, but that's as may be. If they were, they can't have been half as good magicworkers as Aunt Beck. *She* never forgets anything. Ogo was lucky that King Kenig took him in.

Meanwhile Aunt Beck went with her lovely swinging stride and Ogo marched like a pair of scissors beside her, down the hill to the river and across the stepping-stones there, while I came galumphing after.

Dark shapes came out of the fog to us on the other side. "There they are now," said my distant cousin Ivar. We had not seen him for the fog until then. "Ogo seems to have got it right for once. You can strike up now, fellows."

"What is this?" demanded Aunt Beck, standing like a ramrod on the last stepping-stone with brown water swirling below her red heels. But her voice was nearly drowned out by the sudden squeal and chant from the top of the bank as at least four pipers started on the "March of Chaldea."

I was quite as astonished as my aunt. An honor of pipes was quite unheard of at least since the days when we were the Twelve Sisters. But I could now see that there were six pipers up there—more than they had in the castle.

"I said, What is *this*?" my aunt yelled.

"Nothing, my dear cousin. Don't be alarmed," said Ivar. He came right to the bank and offered her his arm. "The King insisted on it for some reason. He said the ladies must be brought in with due honor."

"Humph," said Aunt Beck. But she took his arm and stepped on up the bank. Ivar is a favorite of hers.

I felt better for seeing Ivar there too. He is dark and skinny, with a long neck with a big Adam's apple in it. I consider him very handsome with his beaky, jagged profile, dark eyes, and jutting cheekbones. And he makes good jokes too. Although he doesn't know it yet, I have chosen him to be my husband when the time comes, and until then I feel free to admire him greatly in secret. All the same I wondered, as I scrambled up the bank, what had got into King Kenig, Ivar's father, to escort us with pipers like this. I know the King believes in doing everything the old way, now that Logra is off our backs, but this was ridiculous!

In fact, I was quite glad of those pipers. There is something about a night with no sleep that weakens your legs. It is quite a steep climb up to the castle, and without the steady skirling beat ahead of me I would have made heavy going of it. Or I might not have got there at all. The fog was now so thick that it could have been easy to miss the way, for all I knew it so well.

As it was, I never saw the pipers clearly, just followed them until, under the wet black walls of the castle, they peeled smoothly away, all except one—Old Ian—who led us solemnly up the steps and through into the castle hall.

All was set for dinner there, everyone seated and the servingpeople standing by the walls. There was a lot of yellow light from more candles than I could count. This surprised me greatly. King Kenig is even more fiercely economical than Aunt Beck, and she is a byword for it in the countryside. Old Ian led us solemnly up to the top table, piping the whole way, and stopped when we got there, halfway through the tune.

Ivar dug his elbow into Ogo, and Ogo bowed to King Kenig sitting there. "I—I've brought the ladies to you, sire," he said.

"Round by Kilcannon Head, I imagine. You certainly took your time," the King said. "Get away to your place now."

Ogo turned round with his face very white and the eyes and mouth in it set in straight lines. I have seen him look like that often and often after the children have been jeering at him. Once or twice I have seen him, wearing that same straight face, standing in a lonely part of the castle with tears rushing down his cheeks. As he disappeared to a distant table, I thought the King could have been kinder.

Aunt Beck thought so too. "There is a fog outside," she said.

"Never mind. You're here. Come up, come up," said the King expansively. "Take a seat by me. Both of you."

I was awed. I have eaten at the castle many times, but never at the top table. Ivar had to push me up the step and into a chair. There I sat and stared around. The hall from here looked small and deep, and the tapestries on the walls looked terrible. King Kenig had ordered the wall paintings covered up with embroidery because he said that this was the old way. The trouble was that most of the ladies knew nothing about embroidery and had had to learn as they went along. Their mistakes were very evident in the bright candlelight.

But it was quite possible that Queen Mevenne had arranged it on purpose as a protest. There she sat, along from the empty chair beside the King, looking like a dark night of the soul. She is quite handsome, and her hair is much browner than Aunt Beck's, but she carries with her such an aura of darkness that you could swear she had raven hair and blue skin like a corpse's. Aunt Beck says "Nonsense!" when I tell her this, but I notice she seldom talks to the Queen. The castle children whisper that Queen Mevenne is a witch and murmur of queer doings at the dark of the moon. Aunt Beck says "Nonsense!" to this too, but I am not so sure. It is one drawback to my thoughts of marrying Ivar, knowing I should have a mother-in-law like Mevenne.

Beyond, with another empty chair in between, sat Ivar's elder brother, Donal, heir to the throne, with candlelight shooting ruddy beams from his beard and his ranks of gold bracelets and making a white flash of his teeth as he smiled at something his mother was saying. I do not like Donal either. He looks like a barbarian, but he is a very smooth and clever man indeed.

Beyond Donal and another empty chair was the old Dominie who taught us. His eyebrows were frowning out like crags. . . .

I suppose I should have been wondering about all those empty chairs, but before I begun to think about them properly, pipes sounded again with a dreadful sudden loudness, and to my astonishment King Kenig stood up. Everyone naturally stood up with him. We all looked to the door at the back of the table where a procession came pacing through, following the pipers.

At first all I noticed was a crowd of splendid robes. Then I saw that the foremost of them contained none other than the Priest of Kilcannon, very tall and thin and sour. His eyebrows rival the Dominie's. My heart sank at the sight of him, as it always does. I always have a horrible moment when I think that this man might have been my stepfather had my mother lived. He is the kind who bleaches everything with virtue. But I had never known the King stand to him before. For a moment I wondered if King Kenig had taken up religion as part of his effort to bring back the old ways. Then I saw among the other robes one of red and gold and the elderly, tired man, kind but stately, who was wearing it. He was the only person there in a crown.

"High King Farlane," Aunt Beck murmured beside me. "Ogo might just have warned us."

But Ogo wouldn't, I thought. He had expected us to know. Logra only has the one king, and no one could ever could get it through Ogo's mind that lesser kings like Kenig were any kind of king at all. When Ogo said "the King," he had meant the High King over all Chaldea, naturally, and we had not understood him; even I hadn't, and I had argued with Ogo about it often enough.

When the piping and the grating of chairs and benches stopped, King Farlane was standing behind the special tall carved chair left empty for him.

"We are called here on a matter of justice," he said. "This must be settled before we can go any further. We invoke the favors of all high gods and lesser spirits and thereby open this hearing. Will Kinnock, Priest of Kilcannon, please state his case?"

"I certainly will," the Priest said grimly. "I accuse

Donal, Prince of Conroy and Kilcannon, of robbery, arson, and murder."

"Denied," Donal said calmly, and he turned his arm round to admire the bracelets on it, as if he were a little bored by the matter.

"Denied?" snarled the Priest. His black eyes glared from under his great tufts of black eyebrow. "Do you stand there and have the gall to deny that two nights ago you and your band of ruffians rode up to Kilcannon and set fire to my house?"

Quite a number of people gasped at this, including Ivar. He turned to Donal, glowing with surprise and delight. Ivar shows a regrettable tendency to admire his elder brother. And a childish one. After the first glow Ivar's face went dark and peevish. I heard him mutter, "Why didn't you let me come too?"

"*Answer* me!" thundered the Priest. "Before I bring down the curse of the gods upon you!"

Donal continued to turn bracelets round on his arm. "Oh, I don't deny *that*," he said casually. "It's the charge of robbery and murder I take exception to. Who died?"

"Do you deny you went off with all my sheep? Where are my goats and oxen, you bandit?" raved the Priest. He was shaking with anger so that his fine robe rippled.

"The animals?" said Donal. He shrugged, which made the Priest madder than ever. "We simply drove them off. You'll find them wandering the hills somewhere if you care to go and look."

"You—you—you!" stuttered the Priest.

"I repeat," Donal said. "Who died?"

"A fair question," King Farlane put in. "Was anyone killed?"

The Priest looked as if he had bitten on a peppercorn. "Why, no," he admitted. "I was out with my novices rehearsing for the full moon."

"Then there is no charge of murder to meet," King Farlane pointed out. "And it seems that there was no robbery either. There is only the charge of burning not denied. Prince Donal, what reason had you for burning this man's house?"

"Reason, sire?" Donal said blandly. "Why, I thought the Priest was inside it of course. It is a great disappointment to me to see the wretch strutting in here alive and snarling."

I thought the Priest was going to dance with rage at this. If I had liked Donal more, I would have cheered.

"Sire," said the Priest, "this barefaced wickedness—"

"I object," said Donal, "to being accused of wickedness. What has religion got to do with right and wrong?"

"You sniveling sinner!" thundered the Priest. "Religion has *everything* to do with right and wrong! Let me tell you, Prince, your heathen ways will bring this fair island of Skarr to her knees if—"

"*And* what have my morals to do with politics?" snapped Donal. "What a man does is his own to do, and no concern of the gods or the kingdom."

"This," shouted the Priest, "is the speech of one

who has willfully taken evil to be his good. I denounce you before the High King, your father, and all these witnesses!"

By this time King Kenig—not to speak of most of us standing at the tables—was looking extremely uncomfortable and making little movements as if he wanted to intervene. But the High King stood there, turning his tired, kindly eyes from the Priest's face to Donal's, until the Priest raised both his bony arms and seemed to be going to call curses down on the castle.

"Enough," King Farlane said. "Prince Donal, you are baiting this man. Priest, what damage has the fire done to your house?"

The Priest shuddered to a halt and took his arms down. "Not as much as this evil young man hoped," he said slowly. "It is built of solid stone, roof and all. But the door and window frames, being wood, are mostly burned."

"And what of the inside?" the High King asked gravely.

"Luckily," said the Priest, "the roof sprang a leak

in the rain, and most of it was wet inside. This godless animal threw a brand inside, but it simply charred the floor."

"So what cost would you estimate for repairs?" the High King continued.

"Six ounces of gold," the Priest said promptly. Everyone gasped. "Including the leaking roof," he added.

King Farlane turned to Donal. "Pay him that amount, Prince."

"I protest, sire," said Donal. "He has gold enough off us in temple dues. A more grasping person—"

"Pay him," repeated the King, "and the matter will be thereby settled for good."

"Sire." Donal bowed his head dulcetly and stripped off one of his many bracelets, which he handed to the person next to him at the table. As the bracelet went flashing from hand to hand toward the Priest, Donal said, pretending to be anxious, "Pray have it weighed, Priest. It may be nearer seven ounces."

"No need," said the High King. "The case is concluded."

The Priest received the bracelet, glowering, and it seemed we could all sit down to eat then. But I doubt if the Priest enjoyed his dinner much. He looked sour enough to turn milk.

"Hmm," said Aunt Beck. "Hmm." She took a small rye loaf off a towering basket of them and pushed the basket on to me. "That was all very nicely staged, wasn't it?"

"What do you mean?" I whispered. "Donal and the Priest hate each other, everyone knows that."

"True, but there had to be a glaring reason, I guess, for the High King to come here," my aunt observed. "There will be a private reason too. As we have been specially summoned, we may well discover what it is before long."

"Are you *sure*?" I asked.

"I have in mind," my aunt mused, tearing her loaf apart and reaching for the butter, "two things. First, that our cousin Donal, while addicted to jewelry, seldom wears *quite* so many bracelets. That man can scarcely lift his arms. And second, that I have never known our cousin the King trust Ogo with a message before. Planning lies behind both these things. You'll see."

Blow me down, she was right! We had scarcely finished a splendid dinner, entirely without porridge, to my great joy, and the two kings had scarcely risen and withdrawn to some private place when Donal passed casually along behind our chairs. He was indeed holding his arms rather straight down by his sides. "Ivar," he murmured to his brother, "you and Beck and Aileen follow me, will you?"

We followed, across the platform and out by one of the doors at the back of it. There Donal led us on a corkscrew path through private corridors I did not know and finally up a curving flight of stairs to a heavy door.

"I have given out that Beck and Aileen have gone home," he remarked over his shoulder as he rapped on the door.

"And why, pray?" murmured my aunt, not as if she

expected an answer. I think she was just giving voice to her annoyance that Donal should so coolly organize her movements. Our family is used to come and go as it pleases.

The door was opened by one of the robed attendants of the High King, who stood back and ushered us inside without a word. The room beyond was one I had never seen before, with great windows that, but for the fog, would have given a wide view southward over the sea. As it was, the fog was thinning and giving way to a red sunset, making the light quite confusing, since the room was lit with a tall lamp and many candles.

The High King was sitting with King Kenig on his right and Queen Mevenne on his left. Two more attendants stood in the background, but I scarcely looked at them. The other people in the room were the old Dominie and the Priest of Kilcannon. My heart began to thunder in my ears as I realized that great doings must be afoot, to cause Donal and the Priest to come together in the same small room.

~III~

Ivar was as astonished as I was. "What's going on?" he demanded, making a hasty bow to the two kings.

"Please take a seat," said the High King, "and we shall tell you."

King Farlane was not a well man, I saw as we sat on the low padded stools put ready in front of him. He was huddled in a royal plaid above his scarlet robes, and someone had put a brazier near him for further warmth. But it was his face that showed his illness most. It was white, with a yellowish tinge, and the skin of it was very tight to the bones. What spare flesh there was had drawn into deep wrinkles of pain. But his tired eyes were not subdued by his disease. They gazed at us with a shrewdness and sanity that was almost startling.

"As you know," he said to us—all of us, though I think he spoke chiefly to my aunt—"ten years ago the magicians of Logra cast a spell on our islands of Chaldea so that no one from here, however hard he tries, can get to Logra." He nodded to the Priest, who was so grimly eager to speak that he was sidling in his seat.

"We have tried, gracious King," the Priest burst out. "We have searched the whole of Skarr for some inkling of the spell. We have gone out—I myself have gone out in boats repeatedly—as far as the barrier in the sea, where the boats turn aside as though a current takes them, though there is nothing to be seen. And we have used every craft the gods grant us to break the spell. But we have found no way to break this spell." He subsided, sort of shrinking into himself gloomily. "I have failed," he said. "The gods are not pleased with me. I must fast and pray again."

"There's no need to reproach yourself," King Farlane said.

Donal could obviously not resist muttering, "Och, man, leave your gods to punish you. If they are that angry, they can surely take away your next dinner for themselves."

At this, our old Dominie gave Donal a mildly quelling look and turned his head questioningly to the High King. King Farlane nodded, and the Dominie said, wagging his white eyebrows sadly, "I have had my failures too. It pains me, as a scholar, to say this, but I have now searched in every library on Skarr and journeyed to Bernica to search there too, without stumbling across a single hint of how this spell was constructed."

Oh! I thought. This explained those lovely unexpected days when I had walked to the castle for my lessons to find all the other children rushing around the yard, shouting that Old Dominie was on his travels again.

"On the other hand"—the Dominie continued—
"the clue may lie all around us in the geography of our
very islands."

I sighed. The Dominie had a passion for geography.
He was forever making us draw maps and explaining
to us how the lay of the land influenced history: how
this inlet made a perfect harbor and caused the town to
grow, or how that lone mountain sheltered this valley
and made it so fertile that wars were fought for it. Sure
enough, he went on instructing everyone now.

"As you know," he said, "our three islands form a
crescent with Skarr to the north, Bernica due west, and
Gallis in the south, slanted southeastward, while Logra
forms a very large wedge to the southeast. Now, I have it
in mind that the three Chaldean islands could be seen
to form the sign for the dark of the moon, which also
happens to be the sign for banishment. It would take no
stretch of the imagination for the Lograns to see Logra
as the full moon bearing the shield of banishment
before it. The Lograns, as you know, went to war with

us purely and simply because their gods told them it was their right to conquer Chaldea—"

This was too much for half the people there. They forgot the reverence that should be due to the High King and burst into protest. Donal contented himself with a sarcastic noise, but the Priest unshrank himself and snarled, "The Lograns will burn for their false beliefs!"

Aunt Beck, who was sitting in a demure and graceful attitude on her stool, which I wished I could emulate, with her red heels sweetly together and her bony, sensitive fingers clasped around her knees, tossed her small dark head and very nearly snorted. "There's no gods to it," she said. "It was human greed."

And King Kenig said across her, "Gods, my left hambone, man! Our islands have gold and silver, tin and copper. Gallis has pearls and precious stone as well. What has Logra got? Only iron. And iron makes weapons to conquer the rest with."

The Dominie stuck his lower lip out like a small child, and his eyebrows bristled around at the rest of us. "When one talks of magic," he said huffily, "the impossible is possible."

"Indeed, yes," the High King put in quickly. "Perhaps we should ask what Beck the Wise Woman has to say about the spell."

He looked at my aunt, who bowed her head gracefully back. "Very little, I'm afraid, sire," she said. "Bear in mind that I have had my sister's child to care for and could not be going out in boats or ranging over Skarr. But I have scried and found no answer. I have put bonds on invisible spirits and sent them out all over Skarr."

I watched Aunt Beck doing this. She claimed that all the islands swarmed with spirits, but I still found this hard to believe when I couldn't see them or hear what they reported when they came back.

"They could find nothing of the spell," Aunt Beck said, "and nor could they find any way through to Logra. They all say it's like a wall of glass in the sea between Logra and Chaldea. But they do tell me one thing that worries me. As you know, this world has four great guardians." She looked to the Priest, who pinched his lips in and nodded grudgingly. "These guardians," Aunt Beck said, "belong to north, south, east, and west, but in the nature of things they each have one of our four islands to guard. Ours, as you know, in Skarr is of the North. Bernica is guarded by the West, Gallis by South. Logra *should* have East, but the spell has cut guardian off from guardian so completely that none of our three knows if East even exists anymore."

"That's not important," King Kenig said curtly.

"I regard it as of the utmost importance," Aunt Beck said.

"Well, it may be, it may be," the King conceded. "But the main thing from a king's point of view is that while this magical blockade is in place, the Lograns can build ships and train armies in perfect peace. *And* what is worse, they can send spies through to watch us, while we have no way of spying on them. This is why we're all meeting here in such secrecy: fear of Logran spies."

"It is indeed," the High King agreed, "and of course we may not be seen to build ships or train soldiers because the Lograns hold a most valuable hostage in my son, Alasdair. You are aware of that, are you?" he asked, turning to Ivar and me.

Maybe he thought we were too young to know, since I was three when Prince Alasdair was taken, and Ivar was eight, but I cannot imagine how he thought we didn't know. It was, even Aunt Beck grudgingly agrees, the most astounding piece of magic Logra ever did. She says it must have taken far more planning and clever timing than simply making the barricade. About a year after the barricade was in place, Prince Alasdair—who must have been about Donal's age then—was coming in from hunting with quite a crowd of courtiers when, in the very courtyard of Castle Dromray, which is the High King's seat here on Skarr, a tunnel somehow opened in space and soldiers came rushing in out of nowhere. They shot Prince Alasdair in the leg and then carried off every one of that hunting party, horses and all. People watched from the walls and windows of the castle, quite helpless. Long before they could get down to the courtyard, the tunnel was closed and everyone gone.

I know all about it because my father was one of that hunting party. I nodded. So did Ivar.

"And no news of Prince Alasdair ever after, I believe, sire," Ivar said.

The High King lifted his head and gazed into the coals of the brazier a moment. "As to that," he said, "we are not sure. No, indeed, we are not sure. Rumors, and rumors of rumors, continue to reach us. The last words were so definite that it seems to us and to all our advisors that there must be a crack or so in the wall between Chaldea and Logra."

"And those words are, sire?" asked my aunt.

"That the spell can be breached and Prince Alasdair rescued," the High King answered, "and that the answer can be found if a Wise One journeys from Skarr, through Bernica and Gallis, and enters Logra with a man from each island. This would seem to mean you, my lady Beck."

"It does indeed," my aunt replied dryly, "and where are these words from, sire?"

"From a number of quarters," said King Farlane. "As various as a fishing village at the east of Skarr, word from two of the five kings and queens in Bernica, and two priests and a hermit in Gallis."

"Hmm." My aunt unwrapped her hands from her knees and put her chin in one. "The words always the same?" she asked.

"Almost exactly," said the High King.

There was a moment of silence, in which I wondered what would become of me if Aunt Beck went off to Logra and never came back. The only good thing I could see was that no one would require me to go down to the Place then.

Then, as Aunt Beck drew in breath, almost certainly ready to say "Nonsense!" the High King—whose gift, I was beginning to see, was to put his word in at the right moment—spoke again. He said, "Our plans are made, Wise Beck. You and your apprentice leave secretly this evening. We have a boat waiting for you over the hills in the pool of Illay, and our captain has our orders to sail for Bernica while we and our court journey back to Dromray, giving out that you are with us. This will deceive any spies."

I have seldom seen my aunt discomposed, and never so discomposed as then. Her chin shot up out of her hand. "Go *now?*" she said. She looked from the sick King to the hearty, well one, King Kenig, and then to the Priest, the Dominie, and Donal, sitting admiring his bracelets again. There was almost panic in her face as she realized they were all in this together. She looked up at the expressionless men behind the High King's chair. She even glanced at the Queen, who, like Donal, was playing with a bracelet. "Aileen is too young to go," she said. "She's not even initiated yet."

"She has heard our council," the High King said gently. "If you like, we can take her to Dromray, but she must be closely confined there."

I found my face jumping round from King Farlane to my aunt. It is awful when you sit there thinking the talk is all distant politics and then suddenly find it is going to change your whole life. I was on pins.

"I can't go tonight," my aunt said. "I have no clothes for the journey."

The Queen spoke for the first time, smiling. "We thought of that," she said. "We have clothes already packed for you and Aileen."

Aunt Beck glanced from me to the Queen, but she still gave no indication of what she was going to do with me. Instead she said politely, "Thank you, Mevenne. But I still can't go. I have livestock to feed in my house—six hens, two pigs, and the cow. I can't let them die of neglect."

"We thought of that too," said King Kenig jovially. "My hen woman will take the hens, and Ian the piper will see to the rest. Face it, Beck, you're off to save all Chaldea, woman, even if it is at short notice."

"So I see," said my aunt. She took another unloving

look round the various faces. "In that case," she said, "Aileen goes with me." I was so overwhelmed at this that I only heard it as if from a distance, Aunt Beck adding, "Who is to go with me? Who is the man from the island of Skarr?"

The High King replied, "Prince Ivar is that man, naturally."

I was jolted from my rapt state by Ivar's great, hoarse cry of "Wha-at!"

"You have, like young Aileen, heard all our plans," King Farlane pointed out.

"But," said Ivar, "I only have to set foot in a boat and I get sick as a dog! You *know* I do!" he said accusingly to his mother. He leaped to his feet emotionally. Ivar never conceals his feelings. This is what I admire in him—although I must say at that moment I was less than admiring. His sword whirled as he jumped up and its scabbard hit me quite a thwack on the shoulder.

"Your sword," Donal said, "is for the defense of the

ladies, Ivar. This is your opportunity to behave like a gentleman for once."

Donal is often unkind to his brother. I could see that he was pleased at Ivar's dismay. This is one of the many things I dislike about Donal. But I could see that King Kenig was looking disgusted with his younger son, and the High King, from his carefully neutral expression, was wondering if Ivar was a coward.

I said, rather boldly, as I rubbed my shoulder, "I know we can rely on you, Ivar."

Ivar shot me a dizzy sort of look. "I should have been *warned*," he protested. "To be suddenly told that you're going on a journey—it's—it's—"

King Kenig said, "Don't act the fool, Ivar. The High King has told us how spies from Logra can come and go. There's nothing Logra would like better to hear than that a Prince of Kilcannon is setting out to rescue the High Prince. Utmost secrecy was necessary."

Ivar shot a look at Donal as much as to say why was *he* in the secret then and turned to his mother again.

"Very well, if I *am* to go and I *am* going to be sick, I shall need medicine and a servant to help me."

"A remedy is prepared and packed for you," Queen Mevenne said calmly. I saw Aunt Beck looking a bit sharp at that. Remedies of all kinds are *her* business to provide. But before she could say anything, Ivar's father added, "And Ogo is to go with you as your servant. Now stop this silly noise."

"Ogo!" Ivar exclaimed. "But he's *useless!*"

"Nonetheless," said King Kenig, "Ogo is a Logran and quite likely to be a spy. If you take him with you now without warning, he cannot pass the news on tonight, and you will have him under your eye after."

"Ogo would be as useless as a spy as he is at everything else!" Ivar protested. "Must I really?"

"Yes," said his father. "We are taking no risks."

Here King Farlane stood up, very slowly and weakly, and the rest of us of course had to stand up too. "It only remains," he said, "for us to wish you success on your journey. Go now, in the hands of the gods and"—he looked particularly at Aunt Beck—"for the love of those gods, bring my son back with you if you can."

Aunt Beck ducked him a small, stiff curtsy and looked back at him just as particularly. So did I. The High King was trembling, and strong feelings were trying to stay hidden behind the tight skin of his face. The feelings looked like hope to me—sick, wild hopes of seeing Prince Alasdair again, the kind of hopes that seldom get fulfilled. Aunt Beck saw them too. She had seemed ready to make one of her direst remarks, but instead she said, almost kindly, "I'll do all I can, sire."

⁓IV⁓

After that, we left. One of the High King's robed courtiers came with us to the door, where he passed Aunt Beck a purse. "For expenses," he said.

"Thank you," said my aunt. "I see by this that your king is in earnest." High King Farlane was known to be quite sparing with his money. She turned to Ivar. "Run and fetch Ogo. Tell him just that you and he have to escort the Priest back to his fane."

The Priest was coming with us, to my sorrow, as far as the hilltops where his religious establishment was. Donal went in front of us to show us the way to the small postern I had hardly ever seen used before. For a moment I thought Donal was coming as well. But he was only making sure we found the four little donkeys waiting for us by the wall.

Aunt Beck clicked her tongue at the sight of them. "So much for secrecy. Who saddled these up?"

"I did," Donal said. By the light of the lantern he carried, his teeth flashed rather smugly in his beard. "No chance of any gossip in the stables."

"I was thinking rather," Aunt Beck countered, "of the bags." One donkey was loaded with four leather bags, very plump and shiny and expensive-looking bags. "Who packed these?"

"My mother did," said Donal. "With her own fair hands."

"Did she now?" said Aunt Beck. "Give her my thanks for the honor."

Since no one could have sounded less grateful than my aunt, it was possibly just as well that Ivar came dashing up just then, and Ogo with him, looking quite bewildered. They were to walk, as befitted an escort. The Priest mounted one of the donkeys and sat there looking quite ridiculous with his long legs nearly touching the ground on either side. Aunt Beck sat on the second. Ogo helped me up onto the third. I looked at what I could see of him, which was not much, what with the flickering lantern and the clouds scudding across the nearly full moon, and I thought that no one so puzzled looking and so anxious to help as Ogo could possibly be a spy. Or *could* he?

"You don't have to hold Aileen onto the donkey," Ivar said to him. "Take the baggage donkey's halter and bring it along."

Donal raised the lantern, grinning again, as we all clopped off. "Good-bye, cousins," he said to my aunt and me. "Have a good voyage, Ivar." It was not quite jeering. Donal is too smooth-minded for that. But I thought as we clopped down the rocky hillside that the way he said it amounted to sending us off with a curse—or at least an ill-wishing.

The fog had gone, though my poor little donkey was quite wet with it. It must have been waiting for hours outside that door. All the donkeys were stiff and more than usually reluctant to move. Ivar and Ogo had to take a bridle in each hand and haul them out of the dip below the castle, and go on hauling until we were well set on the path zigzagging to the heights. There my donkey raised its big head and gave voice to its feeling in a huge, mournful "hee-haw!"

"Oh, hush!" I said to it. "Someone might hear."

"It won't matter," said my aunt. In order not to trail her legs like the Priest, she had her knees bent up in front of her. It looked most uncomfortable, and I could see it was making her breathless and cross. "It doesn't matter who hears," she said. "Everyone knows that the Priest must be on his way home." And she called up to the Priest ahead of her on the path, "I am surprised to see you lending yourself to this charade, Kinnock. Why did you?"

"I have my reasons," the Priest called back. "Though

I must say," he added sourly, "I did not expect to have my house burned over it."

"What reasons?" said my aunt.

"The respect for the gods and for the priesthood is not what it should be," he said across his shoulder. "My aim is to set that right."

"You mean you think Alasdair is more god-fearing than his father?" my aunt asked. "If you think that, you're doomed to disappointment two ways."

"Gratitude," retorted the Priest, "is not to be discounted."

"Or counted on either," snapped Aunt Beck.

They continued arguing with Aunt Beck getting crosser and more breathless every sentence, but I have no idea what they said. I remember Aunt Beck accusing the Priest of trying to turn Skarr into Gallis, but that meant they had started to talk politics, and I stopped listening. I was suddenly overwhelmed with a fear that I might not see Skarr again, and I was busy trying to see as much of it as I could by the repeatedly clouded moon.

The mountains were mere blackness overhead, though I could smell the heavy damp smell of them, and the sea was another blackness flecked with white over the other way. But I remember dwelling quite passionately on a large gray boulder beside the path when the moonlight glided over it, and almost as ardently on the gray, wintry-looking heather beneath the boulder. Where the path turned, I could look over my shoulder, across the bent figure of Ogo heaving the luggage donkey's bridle, and see the castle below against the sea, ragged and rugged and dark. There were no lights showing. You'd have thought it was deserted. Of course the house where I lived with Aunt Beck was well out of sight, beyond the next rise of land, but I looked all the same.

It suddenly struck me that if I never saw Skarr again, I would never again need to go down into the Place. You cannot imagine the joy and relief that gave me. Then I found myself not believing this. I knew Aunt Beck would somehow contrive that we gave everyone the slip. We could well be back home again by morning. I knew she was unwilling to go on this unlikely journey—unwilling enough that she might risk the displeasure of the High King himself. As the last and only Wise One in Chaldea, she had standing enough, I thought, to defy King Farlane. Would she dare? *Would* she?

I was still calculating this, with a mixture of excitement and hopelessness on both sides of the question, when we clattered into the deep road at the top of Kilcannon, where the stones of the fane lofted above the shoulder of hill to my right. I could feel them, like an itch or a fizz on my skin and a tendency for the light here to seem dark blue to my eyes. The place makes me so uncomfortable that I hate going near it. Why the gods should require such uncomfortable magics always puzzled me.

A short while later we were out to the flatter land beyond. There stood the Priest's dark house, smelling of burning still, and around it the empty moon-silvered pastures where Donal had driven all the cattle away. On the other side of the road was the long barnlike place where the novices lived. This was brightly lit and—oh, dear!—the most distinct sounds of roistering coming from inside. Evidently the novices had not expected the Priest back until morning.

The Priest leaped down from his donkey and strode to the entrance. A sudden silence fell. Looking through the doorway around the Priest's narrow, outraged body, I could see at least ten young men caught like statues in his glare. Most of them were guiltily trying to hide drinking cups behind their backs, though two were obviously too far gone to bother. One of those went on drinking. The other went on singing and actually raised his cup in toast to the Priest.

"I see," said the Priest, "that the demon drink needs exorcising here. All of you are to walk down to the coast with Wise Beck and see that she gets safely to her boat."

Aunt Beck made a soft, irritated sound. I was right. She had been thinking of slipping off.

"What? Now?" one of the novices asked.

"Yes," said the Priest. "Now." He strode inside the

dwelling and picked up a little barrel from the table, and calmly began pouring its contents on the floor. The scent of whiskey gushed to my nostrils through the door, strong enough to make my eyes water. "Fresh air is a great exorcist," he remarked. "Off you go. And"—he looked at the outside—"I wish you a good journey, ladies."

So we went down the rest of the way with twelve drunken novices. There was quite a strong wind blowing on this side of the mountains, and whatever the Priest said, it seemed to me to make them worse. They wove about, they staggered, they sang, they giggled, and every ten yards or so one of them was sure to pitch forward into a gorse bush while the rest roared with laughter. Several of them had to leave the path to be sick.

"Gods," Ivar kept saying. "This is all I need!"

And Aunt Beck asked them several times, "Are you sure you wouldn't be better sitting down here for a rest? We'll be quite all right on our own."

"Oh, no, lady," they told her. "Can't do that. Orders. Have to shee you shafely to your ship."

Aunt Beck sighed. It was clear the Priest had promised the High King that we would be on that waiting boat. "Drat the man!" said Aunt Beck.

Surrounded by the hooting, galumphing, laughing crowd, we came at last down to where the rocks gave way to sand while the sinking moon showed us quite a large ship swaying up and down vigorously in the bay. Ivar moaned at the sight. Waiting for us among the wet smash and sheen of the breakers was a rowing boat, whose crew leaped out eagerly to meet us.

"Hurry now, or we'll miss this tide," one of them said. "We thought you'd never be here in time."

I slid off the donkey and patted it. I also patted the gorse bush by my side. It was in bloom—but when is gorse not?—and the caress of my fingers released the robust fragrance of it. It is a smell that always makes me think of home and Skarr. It seemed a shame to me that the youngest novice promptly staggered into that same bush and was sick on it.

"Here, lassie." One of the sailors seized me and

swung me into his arms. "Carry you through the water," he explained when I uttered a furious squawk.

I let him. I became almost unbearably tired just then. It seemed to me that in leaving the soil of Skarr I left all my strength behind, but I expect that it was just that I'd had no sleep the night before. As I was carried through the crashing surf, tasting salt as I traveled, I had glimpses of Ivar and Ogo wading beside me and a further glimpse of Aunt Beck, drawn up to her very tallest, facing the sailor who had offered to carry her too. I saw her glance at the waves, lift a heel and glance at that, and then shrug and give in. She rode to the boat sedately sitting across the sailor's arms, heels together and both hands clasped demurely round his neck, as if the poor man were another donkey.

I scarcely remember rowing out to the big dark boat. I think I must have been asleep before they got there. When I woke, it was bright gray morning and I was lying on my face, on a narrow bench in a warm but smelly wooden cabin. I sprang up at once. I knew it was only a matter of forty sea miles to Bernica.

"Heavens!" I cried out. "I've missed the whole voyage!"

It turned out to be no such thing. When I dashed out into the swaying, creaking passage under the deck, Aunt Beck met me with the news that we had met contrary winds in the night. "The sailors tell me," she said, "that the Logra barricade diverts the air and the sea too when the wind is in the north. We shall be a day or more yet on the way." And she sent me back to do my hair properly.

Breakfast was in a little bad-smelling cubbyhole at the stern, where the sea kept smashing up against the one tiny window and the table slid up and down like a seesaw. No porridge, to my surprise. I wouldn't have minded porridge. I was ravenous. I laid into oatcakes and honey just as if we were on dry land and the honey pot didn't keep sliding away down the table whenever I needed it.

After a while Aunt Beck wiped her fingers and passed the cloth to me. "Ten oatcakes is plenty, Aileen," she told me. "This ship doesn't carry food for a month. Go and see what has become of Ivar and Ogo."

I went grudgingly. I wanted—apart from more oatcakes—to go on deck and see the sea. I found the boys in a fuggy little space across the gangway. Ivar was lying on the bed, moaning. Ogo sat beside him, looking anxious and loyal, holding a large bowl ready on his knees.

"Go *away*!" said Ivar. "I'm dying!"

Ogo said to me, "I don't know what to *do*. He's been like this all night."

"Go and fetch Aunt Beck," I said. "Get some breakfast. I'll hold the bowl."

Ogo passed me the bowl like a shot. I put it on the floor. It was disgusting.

"Don't put it there!" Ivar howled as Ogo dashed from the room. "I *need* it! Now!" He did look ill. His face was like suet, all pale and shiny. I picked up the bowl again, but he wailed, "I've nothing left to be sick with! I'll *die*!"

"No, you won't," I said. "It's not heroic. Where's the medicine your mother packed for you?"

"In the bag you're sitting on," Ivar gasped. "But stupid Ogo doesn't know which it *is*!"

"Well, I don't suppose I do either," I said, getting up and opening the bag, "and I'm not stupid. Why don't *you* know?"

Ivar just buried his face in the lumpy little pillow and moaned. Luckily Aunt Beck came in just then. "This is ridiculous," she said, taking in the situation. "I thought Ogo was exaggerating. Move over, Aileen, and let me have a look in that bag."

There were quite a number of jars and bottles in the bag, carefully packed among clothes. Aunt Beck took them all out and arranged them in a row on the floorboards. "Hmm," she said. "Which?" She picked up the glass bottles one by one and held them up against the light. She shook her head. She picked up the earthenware jars one by one, took the corks out, and sniffed. Ivar reared up on one elbow and watched her anxiously. Aunt Beck shook her head again and, very carefully and deliberately, began pouring the contents away into the bowl.

"Hey!" said Ivar. "What are you *doing*?"

"I do not know," Aunt Beck said, starting to empty the glass bottles into the bowl too, "what Mevenne was intending here, but I fear she is as bad at remedies as she is at embroideries. Aileen, take this bowl up on deck and empty it all into the sea. Be careful not to spill it on the way. It could set fire to the ship. Then come back for the bottles. They need to be thrown overboard too."

"But what shall I *do*?" Ivar was wailing as I carried the bowl away as carefully and steadily as I could.

Aunt Beck snapped at him to behave himself and to take that filthy shirt off at once.

It took me quite a while to get that bowl poured away. I was two steps along the gangway when the ship pitched sideways, suddenly and violently. And do what I could, the bowl swilled and slopped some of the stuff on the wooden floor. There was only the merest drop, but it made a truly horrible smell and started to smoke. Aunt Beck had not been joking about those medicines. I went the rest of the way more carefully than I had ever done anything in my life. I put the bowl down on each step of the wooden stair that went up to the deck and held it steady as I climbed after it. I crept with it out into the sudden brisk daylight on deck. There were ropes everywhere, sailors staring, and a dazzle of choppy waves beyond. But I kept my eyes grimly on the nasty liquid in the bowl the whole way to the edge of the boat and carefully looked which way the wind was before I started to pour the stuff away. I didn't want it blowing back in my face. It was a huge relief when I finally tipped the bowlful into the brownish rearing waves.

The sea boiled white where the liquid went in. I had to wait for the ship to move past the whiteness before I could lie on my front and swill the bowl out. That made a lesser whiteness. I snatched my hand away and, I am afraid, lost the bowl, which dipped and sank almost at once. Oh well, I thought. Probably good riddance.

When I went back below, the spilled drop had stopped smoking, but there was a round charred place where it had been.

In the cabin Ivar was now sitting up, his top half all gooseflesh without his shirt, staring at Aunt Beck. Aunt Beck had taken her ruby-ended pin out of her hair and was wagging it slowly in front of Ivar. "Watch the pin. Keep watching my pin," she was saying, but broke off to pass me the bottles and jars all bundled up in Ivar's shirt. "Overboard," she said. "Shirt and all."

"Hey!" said Ivar. "That's a good shirt!" He stopped staring at Aunt Beck and scowled at me.

"Curses," said Aunt Beck. "Have to begin again. Ivar, *attend* to this pin of mine."

It took very little time to get rid of the bundle. When I got back this time, Ivar was staring at Aunt Beck, looking as if he had suddenly gone stupid. Aunt Beck was saying, "Say this after me now: 'I am a good sailor.

I never get seasick.' Go on—'I am a good sailor . . .'"

Ivar said obediently, "I am a good sailor. I never get seasick."

"A *very* good sailor," Aunt Beck prompted. "No weather affects me, ever."

"*Very* good sailor," Ivar repeated. "No weather affects me, ever."

"Good." Aunt Beck snapped her fingers in front of Ivar's eyes, then sat back on her heels and stared at him closely. Ivar blinked and shifted and gazed around the small, dim cabin. "How are you now?" Aunt Beck asked, handing him a clean shirt.

Ivar looked at her as if he were not all that sure for a moment. Then he seemed to come to life. "Ow!" he said. "By the Guardians, I'm *hungry!*"

"Of course you are," Aunt Beck agreed. "You'd better run along and get breakfast before Ogo eats all the oatcakes."

"Gods of Chaldea!" Ivar leaped up. "I'll kill him if he has!" Clutching his shirt to his front, he pounded away to the eating room. Aunt Beck climbed to her feet and pushed her ruby pin back into her hair, looking satisfied. Quite smug, really.

I was going to follow Ivar, in case he did attack Ogo. You can never trust Ogo to defend himself properly. But Aunt Beck stopped me. "Not now," she said. "We've work to do. I want to know what Mevenne packed in *our* bags."

I sighed a little and followed her across the gangway. The bags were piled at one end of our cabin. Aunt Beck knelt down and unbuckled the top one. A strong smell came out. It was not exactly a bad smell, rather like chamomile and honey gone bad, only not quite. It made me feel a little seasick. Aunt Beck bit off a curse and clapped the bag shut again.

"Up on deck with these," she said to me. "You take those two, Aileen."

I did as she said, but not easily. Those bags were good-quality hide, and heavy. I thought Aunt Beck was going to throw them into the sea. But she stopped in the shelter of the rowing boat, where it was roped to the deck, and dumped the bags down there.

"Put yours here," she said to me, kneeling down to open one, "and then we shall see. What have we here?" She pulled out a grand-looking linen gown and unfolded it carefully. There were brown twiggy bits of herb in every fold. "Hmm," she said, surveying and sniffing. Her face went very stiff. For a moment she simply knelt there. Then she put her head up cheerfully and said to me, "Well, well. Mevenne was no doubt trying to keep moths away and has got it wrong as usual. Take each garment as I hand it to you and shake it out over the side. *With* the wind, mind. Make sure none of these unfortunate plants touch the ship or yourself either if you can avoid it." And she bundled the gown into my arms.

It took me half an hour to shake all the herbs away. Aunt Beck passed me garment after fine garment, each still folded, each stuffed with herbs like a goose ready for roasting. Some of the woolen ones took no end of shaking because the twiggy bits stuck into the fabric and clung there. About halfway through I remember asking, "Won't this poison the sea, Aunt Beck?"

"No, not in the least," Aunt Beck replied, lifting out underclothes. "There is nothing like salt water to cancel bad magics."

"Even if it was unintentional?" I asked.

Aunt Beck smiled a grim little smile. "As to that . . . ," she said, and then said nothing more, but just passed me a bundle of underclothing.

By the end we had a heap of loose clothing and four empty bags. Aunt Beck knelt on the heap, picking up shirts and sleeves, sniffing and shaking her head. "Still smells," she said. "These are such fine cloth that it goes against the grain with me to throw them in the sea too. Kneel on them, Aileen, or they'll blow away, and I'll see what I can do."

She went briskly away and came back shortly with a coil of clothesline and a basket of pegs. Goodness knows where she had got them from. Then we both became very busy slinging up the line around the deck and pegging out flapping garments all over the ship. Ivar and Ogo came up on deck to stare. The sailors became very irritable, ducking under clothing as they went about their work and sniffing the bad chamomile scent angrily.

Eventually the Captain came and accosted Aunt Beck, under a billowing plaid. "What are you *doing* here, woman? This is a fine time to have a washday!"

"I'm only doing what needs doing, Seamus Hamish," Aunt Beck retorted, pegging up a wildly kicking pair of drawers. "This clothing is contaminated."

"It surely is," said the Captain. "Smells like the devil's socks. Are you raising this wind to blow the smell away?"

Aunt Beck finished pegging the drawers and faced the Captain with her red heels planted well apart and her arms folded. "Seamus Hamish, I have never raised wind in all my born days. What would be the need on Skarr? What is the need here?"

Seamus Hamish folded his arms too. It was impressive because his arms were massive and covered with pictures. "Then it is the smell doing it."

Whatever was doing it, there was no doubt that the wind was getting up. When I looked out from under the flapping clothing, I could see yellow-brown waves chopping up and down and spume flying from the tops of them. Aunt Beck actually had long black pieces of hair blowing from her neatly plaited head. "Nonsense!" she said, and turned away.

"I tell you it is!" boomed the Captain. "And turning the sky purple. Look, woman!" He pointed with a vast arm, and sure enough, the bits of sky I could see were a strange hazy lilac color.

Aunt Beck said, "Nonsense, man. This is the barrier doing it." She picked up one of the bags and began punching and pounding it to turn it inside out.

"I have never seen the sky this color," Seamus Hamish declared. "And you must take at least this plaid down. My steersman can't see his road for it."

"Aileen," said Aunt Beck, "take the plaid and peg it somewhere else."

I did as I was bid. The only other place I could find was a rope on the front of the ship. I got Ogo to help me because the wind was now so fierce that I couldn't hold the plaid on my own. We left it flying out from the prow like a strange flag and went back to find Aunt Beck had turned all the bags inside out and was strapping them to the rowing boat to air. The ship's cook was looming over her.

"And if you didn't take my basin, who did?" he was saying.

Ogo and I exchanged guilty looks. Ogo had fetched the basin for Ivar, and I had dropped it into the sea.

Aunt Beck shrugged. "None of my doing, man. The Prince of Kinross was unwell in the night. The bowl is now unfit to cook with."

The cook turned and glared at Ivar, who was leaning against one of the masts with his hair blowing, looking very fit and rosy. He stared back at the cook in a most princely way. "My apologies," he said loftily.

"Then I must mix my dough some other way, I suppose," the cook said grumpily. And he went away muttering, "Always bad luck to sail with a witch. The curse of Lone on you all!"

Aunt Beck didn't seem to hear, which was lucky. Nothing enrages her more than being called a witch. She simply got up and went below to tidy her hair.

"What is the curse of Lone?" Ogo asked me anxiously as we stood among the flapping garments. They were flapping more and more as the wind rose. The ship was pitching, and waves were hissing against the deck.

I had never heard of the curse, but Ivar said, "Obvious. It means that you disappear like the Land of Lone did."

The words were hardly out of his mouth when there was a grinding and a jolting from underneath, followed by a crunching from somewhere up at the front. The ship tilted sideways and seemed to stop moving. Above the noise of several huge waves washing across the deck, I could hear Seamus Hamish screaming curses at the steersman and the steersman bawling back.

"You slithering blind ass's rear end! *Look* what you did!"

"How is a man to steer with that woman's washing in his face? All I could see was her drawers flapping!"

"I wish you hadn't said that about the curse," I shouted at Ivar. "I think we've run into the barrier."

"It was the cook made the curse, not me!" he yelled back. He was hanging on to the mast. Ogo and I clutched at the rowing boat. We all had seawater swilling around our ankles.

V

But we had not run into the barrier. When Aunt Beck shot back on deck, still pinning her plait up around her head, she said, "Ah, I thought as much from the color of the sea. We're into a piece of the lost land here."

As the Dominie had so often told us, there was a line of reefs and rocks in the sea between Logra and Skarr that were all that remained of the Land of Lone after it broke up and sank in the earthquake. The Dominie had sailed out to see it for himself when he was young, and he said that there was ample proof that it had once been inhabited. He had found broken crockery and pieces of fine carving lodged among the rocks. Sailors told him that some of the longer skerries even had remains of buildings on them. Ogo was always very impressed by this.

"The Dominie told us all about it," he said excitedly to Aunt Beck. "He found a carved comb and most of a fine vase. Can we go and look, do you think?"

"Oh, shut up! Who cares?" Ivar said.

"But I always wondered—" Ogo started again.

By this time Seamus Hamish was bawling for us all to climb off onto the rocks to lighten the ship, so that he could get us afloat again and see what the damage was. The poor ship was grinding back and forth, back and forth, which sounded very dangerous, and sailors were already ducking under the clotheslines with boxes and bundles of cargo, to lower them carefully overboard. Some of them stopped and helped us down too. Ogo was so eager that he jumped down by himself in a great floundering leap.

"And the sea all round the Lost Land is always brown

with its earth," I heard him saying, while the cook was passing me down into someone's big tattooed arms.

Ivar, of course, could not be outdone by Ogo. He leaped by himself too, and landed with a clatter and twisted his ankle and complained about it for the next hour. And Aunt Beck went down as she had come aboard, peacefully riding another sailor.

"There will be no damage," she said to me as she was carried past me. "Can they not trust me to protect the ship I sail in?"

Her sailor dumped her up beyond the rocks in a very expressive No Comment way. I ambled along to where she was and found that the place we had run into was really quite a large island, sandy and rocky and desolate under the queer hazy lilac sky. There was a bit of cliff ahead about as tall as Ogo, and above that, there seemed to be some trees.

"Can we explore?" Ogo was asking eagerly. "How long do we have?"

"I'll see," said Aunt Beck.

I looked back at the poor ship as Aunt Beck called over to the Captain. There it was, lying sideways and grinding, grinding, between two prongs of rock and hung all over with colored clothing. Very undignified. Seamus Hamish was busy getting the sails in, but he yelled back that we could have an hour. And he told the cook and another sailor to go with us.

"I shall stay here," Ivar said. "My ankle really hurts."

We left him sitting on a rock surrounded in yellow sea foam while we made for the cliffs. I was quite as eager as Ogo was. The Dominie had said that the earthquake had happened over a thousand years ago, and as far as I knew, I had never seen anywhere that old. Aunt Beck was, as always, demure and restrained, but she seemed to me to be springing up the cliff as eagerly as any of us. It was one of the easiest climbs I have ever made, although I must confess that my good dress suffered a little on the way.

Halfway up, Ogo said, "Hey! What's this?" and picked up something that looked like a big broken saucepan lid. It seemed to be made of very old black leather. We all gathered on a crumbly ledge to examine it. You could still see that there had been patterns stamped on it.

Aunt Beck had just taken the thing to hold the patterns to the light when Ivar came scrambling limpingly up beside us.

"Ogo," he said, "you're supposed to be my *servant*. You're supposed to *stay* with me. You know I've hurt my ankle. What are you doing going off and picking up rubbishing old shields for?"

"It *was* a shield, I think," Aunt Beck said, turning the thing around. She has beautifully shaped artistic fingers. I am always impressed when she handles things. "These patterns—" she said.

"Throw it away," said Ivar.

"No, don't," said the cook. "I can sell it on Bernica. They like old things there."

"These *patterns*," Aunt Beck said loudly, "are the symbols of the Guardian of the North. Put it back where you found it, Ogo. It is something none of us should meddle with."

She was probably right. I had last seen symbols like that embroidered on High King Farlane's robe. Everyone watched, rather chastened, while Ogo carefully put the broken shield back on the ledge where he had found it. "I could have got a hundred silver for that," the cook remarked as we all went on up the cliff.

The cook looked very glum at that and said nothing more until we arrived among the trees at the top. There it was as if the whole ground ran away from us. Tiny creatures—mice, rats, voles—sped and scuttled out of our way. I saw rabbits, squirrels, a weasel, and even a beast like a small deer running from us among the trees. Small birds and large ones clapped out of the tops of the wood. None of the trees was tall. They were all bent and bowed in the sea wind, but I could see they were trees that were very rare on Skarr, like elders and hazels, and were just coming into leaf. Aunt Beck put up an elegant hand to old dusty catkins and then to the light green beginnings of elder flowers. The other sailor said, "I wish I'd brought my crossbow! Fat pigeons. That deer."

"Fine rabbits," agreed the cook, and Ivar said, "Let's go back. There's nothing here. My ankle hurts."

"We shall go on," Aunt Beck decreed. "I want to see how big this place is."

"I want to know how all these animals got here," I said.

"Well, you won't find that out by walking about," Ivar said. "My ankle—"

"The animals," Aunt Beck said, "undoubtedly descend from creatures that fled from the earthquake. Ah, we're getting somewhere."

The trees gave way to big rocks and fluttering grass. I saw harebells there. We went round the largest boulder and saw the sea again beyond us, angrily crashing below on whole piles of rocks. In the distance you could actually see the barrier, like a band of white mist that stretched away in both directions as far as anyone could see. Nobody looked at it, though, because there were the remains of buildings in front of us. The walls were not quite as high as my head and made of blocks of sandy-colored stone. There were beautifully chiseled patterns on them.

"Oh, good!" I said. Now we were definitely one up on the Dominie. He had only *heard* of buildings; we were actually looking at some.

Ogo led the way in through the nearest broken opening. Aunt Beck and I followed quite as eagerly, and the sailors plunged in after us, staring round in a mixture of interest and hope that there might be something they could sell on Bernica. Ivar limped behind, complaining about his ankle.

It was like a labyrinth. We went this way and that into square spaces and oblong ones, where it was almost impossible to tell whether we were going through rooms or across courtyards. In one space there was a definite fireplace in the wall. It was surrounded with beautiful broken green and blue tiles, and carving outside those. There was even the remains of soot on the piece of chimney that was left. The tiles had the same symbols on them that we had seen on the broken shield.

"This was a room, then!" Ogo said.

The cook slyly tried to prize a piece of tile away. Aunt Beck turned and *looked* at him, and he hastily took his hand away. He followed us, muttering about damn witches, and Ivar followed him, muttering about his ankle.

We went through spaces with mysterious pits in the ground and a square with a round pool of water in the middle and another with a regular round hillock in the center. Ogo chattered to Aunt Beck the whole way, trying to work out what the spaces had once been. To my disappointment, Aunt Beck had no idea more than the rest of us. And Ivar never stopped complaining.

I got really annoyed with him. "Ivar," I said, "just shut up, will you! You sound utterly ignoble!"

"But my ankle *hurts*," he said.

"Then bear it. Behave like a prince should," I said.

"I—" he began. Then he shut his mouth with a gulp. He stopped complaining, but he hobbled worse than ever and glowered at me whenever I looked at him.

He's been spoiled all his life, I thought. I must start training him to be a good husband while he's away from Mevenne. She can't have been a good influence.

This was just before we came out into a flat, round space with the broken remains of pillars regularly around it. The pillars were taller than any of us, but they did not look so tall because they were surrounded by bushes of a kind I had never seen before, glossy-leaved and laden with small white flowers. A gust of fine sweet scent blew in the wind from them.

"Ah, I have it," Aunt Beck said to Ogo. "This was once a temple. Those are kemmle bushes. They grow them in the great fane at Dromray, too."

"What are the rest of the buildings, then?" Ogo wanted to know as we threaded our way through the bushes.

As we came out into open pavement in the middle of the circle, Aunt Beck said, "How am I to tell? The priests needed somewhere to live, I suppose."

There was a cry from above us. We all looked

upward. The ugliest cat I had ever beheld was bounding gladly from pillar to pillar toward us. He was pale-furred and marked in gray stripes and splotches and all legs and angles, with a long, skinny tail like a snake. His ears were too big for his flat, triangular face. His eyes were huge and green-blue like the tiles on the broken fireplace. But he growled with pleasure at the sight of us, and when he came to the nearest pillar, he jumped down—the way that cats do, reaching with his forepaws first as far down as he could and then risking a leap— and crashed in among the bushes. As he came crashing out and trotted toward us, we saw he was huge for a cat, at least as big as King Kenig's deerhounds.

The sailor said, "Why didn't I bring my bow?" and backed away. Ivar hid behind Ogo, which meant that Ogo couldn't back away, though I could see he wanted to. He said in a shaky voice, "What a plug-ugly creature!"

"True," said Aunt Beck. "But not fierce, I think."

He came trotting straight up to me, for some reason,

and I could hear him purring as he came, like someone rasping a file on a stone. I bent down and rubbed his ears and face, just the way I would have rubbed one of the castle wolfhounds. The cat loved it. His purr became a rumble. He pushed himself against me and wrapped his tail around my legs. Close to, his coat had a sort of pink look, as if his skin were showing through. "You *are* a plug-ugly," I said to him, "but you must be awfully lonely here."

"Oh, he's bound to have a mate somewhere," Aunt Beck said, and went to have a closer look at the pillars. They didn't seem to tell her much.

"Let's go," Ivar said. "This place is boring."

Aunt Beck looked round for the sun, which was quite high, beaming through the strange lilac haze. "Yes," she said. "I wouldn't put it past Seamus Hamish to leave without us." She turned to go, and stopped, quite unusually unsure. "Do you remember where we came in?" she said to Ogo.

At that, they all milled about, bewildered, except

for me. I was kneeling down by then with my arms round Plug-Ugly. He was so sturdy and soft and warm and he had so obviously taken to me that I didn't care how ugly he was. "Do *you* know the way out of here?" I asked him.

And he did. He turned and trotted between two of the pillars, where there was a gap in the bushes and a faint narrow path beyond that. I think he must have made that path himself, going hunting over the years.

"This way!" I called to the others. "The Lone Cat knows." I don't know why I called him that, except that it seemed right for his official name. Plug-Ugly was his private name, between him and me.

They all followed us rather dubiously, Ivar saying we could hardly be lost on such a small island and sounding as if he thought we were. The path took us out to a rocky shoulder on the other side of the temple place and then down and around, until we could see the ship below us. It looked far more normal now. They had taken Aunt Beck's clotheslines down as well as the sails and launched the rowing boat. A team of oarsmen was in the rowing boat, towing the ship backward out of the rocks.

Ivar at once forgot all about his ankle and went racing down the hill, shouting to the sailors to wait. The cook and our sailor pelted after him, bellowing that we were ready to come aboard now. Aunt Beck came stepping neatly down among the rocks, looking ominous. Ogo sort of hovered in front of her. I could see Seamus Hamish glowering up at us from the stern of the ship.

When Plug-Ugly and I arrived, Aunt Beck was saying, "You'll not have thrown those good garments in the sea, I trust."

Seamus Hamish dourly pointed to where the clotheslines and the clothes lay in a jumbled heap by the forward mast. "Make haste aboard," he said. "We'll not be waiting for you."

Everyone scrambled up into the ship, so quickly that I can't remember how Aunt Beck arrived there. The oarsmen went on rowing all the while, so that when it came to my turn to get aboard, there was quite a wide, seething gap between rocks and ship. Plug-Ugly roved up and down in front of it, uttering long, dismal mewings.

"He wants to come with us," I called to Aunt Beck. "*Could* he?"

"No way am I having an ill-fated creature like that on my ship," Seamus Hamish shouted, storming across the deck. "Get gone, creature! Shoo!" And he waved menacingly at Plug-Ugly, who was looking miserable.

Aunt Beck shrugged. "I'm sorry, my good beast," she said. "The Captain has spoken. Catch hold of my hand, Aileen, and I'll pull you over." She held out her hand, and I just managed to catch hold of it and just managed a long, long stride to get one foot aboard. Aunt Beck pulled me the rest of the way. I turned round and watched Plug-Ugly sitting there, growing smaller as the sailors rowed us triumphantly out to sea.

I wept. "Oh, sorry, sorry!" I called out to Plug-Ugly. He looked a Lone Cat indeed sitting there in the distance.

"Pull yourself together," Aunt Beck said to me. "He's lived in that temple for years, perfectly happily. He'll soon forget you. Come and help me untangle this mess the sailors have made of our clothing."

Seamus Hamish would not allow us to do this on deck. He said the sailors needed to get the rowing boat in and hoist the sails, and he made us take the whole bundle downstairs into the breakfast cubbyhole. He sent Ivar and Ogo down there with us to get them out of the way too. They sat and watched while we disentangled a fine warm-looking green dress.

"That looks to be about your size," Ivar remarked to me. "I wonder where Mother got it?"

"Can I wear it now?" I asked Aunt Beck.

She looked from the dress to me. My best dress was torn and stained with tar from the deckboards and seawater, and in addition, Plug-Ugly had smeared it all over with his long pinkish hairs. "Hmm," she said. She turned the green dress this way and that, sniffed it, and finally passed it to me. "Go and put it on in our cabin," she told me. "Tidy your hair while you're at it."

I went off almost cheerfully. It was not often I got a fine new dress like this one. It almost made up for having to leave Plug-Ugly, I thought as I opened the cabin door.

The first thing I saw there was Plug-Ugly himself. He was stretched out along my bunk, pretty well filling it, busy eating a fat dead rat. He looked up and burst out purring when he saw me.

"How did you— No, I won't ask," I said. "It has to be magic. Plug-Ugly, I'm *really* happy to see you, but do you mind eating that rat on the floor?"

Plug-Ugly gave me a wide sea green stare. I had resigned myself to a ratty bed that night, when he tossed the rat playfully over his shoulder, the way cats do. It flew across the cabin and landed on Aunt Beck's bunk.

"Oh, well," I said. I took off my spoiled dress and gave it to him to lie on. He liked that. He lay on it and purred, while I hooked myself into the pretty green one. "Move that rat," I told him as I left. "You don't know

Aunt Beck. She'll give you what for if you leave it there!"

"Hey, that looks good!" Ogo said shyly. He was coming along the corridor with his arms full of our inside-out bags. "The Captain was going to keep these," he told me. "He was really annoyed when I asked for them."

All I could think of to say was "Hmm," like Aunt Beck does. I was glad the dress looked good, but what *was* going on with this voyage? We had been given contaminated clothes and poisonous medicine and a Captain who would happily have left us stranded on that island. But surely Kenig and Mevenne didn't want to lose their own son. Did they? But Donal would love to be rid of his brother, I thought. He had never liked Ivar. And Donal had definitely been plotting something, back on Skarr.

Aunt Beck was certainly thinking along the same lines. She looked up from precisely folding underclothes to say, "Thank you, Ogo. Aileen, you forgot to tidy your hair." And then, after a pause: "Ivar, Ogo, do either of you have any money?"

They both looked alarmed. Ogo patted his pockets and found a copper penny. Ivar dug around in *his* pockets and found two silvers and three coppers.

"And I have precisely one half silver," Aunt Beck said.

"What do you need it for?" Ivar asked. "I thought King Farlane's chancellor gave you a purse."

"It is full of nothing but stones, with a few coppers on top to conceal the trick, and someone," said Aunt Beck, "has to pay Seamus Hamish for this voyage. Even if your father has already done so, we shall still need to buy food and pay for lodging when we get to Bernica. I must think what to do."

The fine clothes, still smelling of not-quite-honey and chamomile, were neatly packed back in the bags. I was just buckling them up when the cook arrived with our lunch. It was pickled herrings and soda bread.

"I can't give you more or better," he said in his gruff way. "Captain's found his temper again, seeing as we have the barrier in view and can follow it south to

Bernica, but says we'll be another day on the way. We didn't load food enough for all this voyaging."

"I see," Aunt Beck said calmly. "This will do well enough for now." And as the cook was leaving, she asked, even more calmly, "I suppose poor Seamus Hamish gets little or no payment for carrying us all to Dunberin this way?"

The cook stopped in the doorway. "Why do you ask?"

"I meant—seeing he has to economize with the food," said Aunt Beck.

The cook swung round, looking very sincere and earnest. "Ah, no," he said. "That was my miscalculation, you'll understand. His temper's up already over that. He likes to eat well, the Captain. And seeing the High King has promised him a bag of gold for landing you safe in Holytown and King Kenig has promised him another when we return to Skarr without you, the Captain told me to lay in lavishly, which I thought I had."

"Indeed?" said Aunt Beck. "Since that is the way of it, we must all accept the situation. Thank you."

As soon as the cook had gone, Ivar burst out, "The thieving, money-grabbing skinflints! They're promised two bags of gold and they feed us *this*!" He pointed at the herrings, and I swear his eyes popped with rage.

"It will fill you up," said Aunt Beck, sharing round the food. "Although," she added pensively, "I would like to see what the good Captain is eating at this moment."

"Venison," Ogo said glumly. "I smelled it cooking."

"And why are they going to drop us in Holytown and not Dunberin?" Ivar demanded. "It's *miles* farther down the coast."

"It seems King Farlane ordered it," Aunt Beck said. "And I expect it has something to do with whisky as well. We should be thankful, Ivar. Holytown is not a large place, like Dunberin, and should be less expensive. Remember, we have next to no money."

But when the meal was over, she took me into our cabin on the pretext of putting the bags in there. "Aileen," she said, turning very serious, "I didn't wish to say this in front of those two boys, but I am very much afraid that your cousin King Kenig did not intend us to survive this journey."

I had been nervously searching the tiny space for Plug-Ugly. There was no sign of him, or the rat either. I was beginning to wonder if I had dreamed him, when Aunt Beck spoke. It jerked my attention back to her. "But what shall we do?" I said. "Do you think that this prophecy about Prince Alasdair is false, then?" And a shameful thing it was, I thought, that someone was playing with King Farlane's hopes.

"It could be," said my aunt. "Prophecies are sly, chancy things and easy enough to invent. I'll keep an open mind there. But it may just be someone—Donal or Mevenne, for instance—seizing a chance when it offered. As to what we *do*, well, child, first, we keep Ivar safe, and second, we try to get to Logra the way they want us to, and being forewarned, then we'll see."

⌁ VI ⌁

Holytown was a little low gray town with an irregular stone jetty. From the moment we reached it, it was all confusion. The Captain couldn't wait to get rid of us. Our bags were thrown out on the jetty almost before the ship was tied up, and we found ourselves following them into a frenzy of fish and shouting. We seemed to have arrived just as the fishing fleet came in. All around us silver streams of fish were being poured into barrels, or laid out in boxes, or being bought and sold out of deep smelly holds. Bernica people are not very tall. It added to my confusion that Aunt Beck and Ogo towered out of the crowd, and even I found I was nearly as tall as most people around me.

"I'm starving," said Ivar. "Can we buy some?"

"Not at these prices," Aunt Beck said. She was staring keenly around, evidently looking for something.

Ogo nudged me and pointed. Just for an instant I had a sight of Plug-Ugly rubbing himself against the legs of a little person in green robes. He was gone again as I looked.

At the same moment Aunt Beck said, *"Ah!"* and strode toward the green robes.

There was a whole group of them ambling cheerfully among the fish, pausing to bargain and then moving on with a fish or two in their baskets. They did not look very well-to-do. All the green robes were frayed and grubby. The men mostly went barefoot; the women had homemade-looking sandals. But the oddest thing about them was that each of them had an animal or a bird. I saw a squirrel on one man's shoulder, and one woman had a rabbit nestled in her basket alongside the fish. Somebody else was leading a sheep, and another seemed to have a fox.

"Who are they, Aunt?" I asked as Aunt Beck surged purposefully toward them.

"Monks and nuns," she replied. "They worship the Lady."

This left me very little wiser. Nothing could have been more unlike the Priest of Kilcannon and his novices. As we came up with the group, I found myself surrounded by cheerful faces and strange beasts. I assumed the nun nearest me had an odd black-feathered headdress until the headdress turned a round yellow eye on me and went, "Craark!" And I realized she had a raven sitting on her green hat. "His name's Roy," she said. "He'll not hurt you. And what will you folks be wanting?"

"Your help, brothers and sisters," Aunt Beck said. "We need to be directed to the King."

"The King!" said several of them, rather astonished. And one little fat man asked, "And why would you be wanting the King?" He was perhaps the oddest of all the monks because he had a beard that grew in two long wisps, one wisp from each cheek, that were long enough to be tucked into the rope he wore as a belt. On his shoulder sat a truly magnificent green bird— shiny green with an arched beak and round yellow eyes even more knowing than the raven's. Each eye was surrounded in wise pinkish wrinkles that made it look very clever indeed. The long, long green tail swept down the little monk's back like a waterfall even longer than the monk's wispy beards.

And it spoke. Ogo, Ivar, and I all jumped when it said, in a loud, squawking voice, "It's Thursday! It's Thursday!"

"Oh, and so it is!" said the nun with the raven. "Green Greet is quite right."

"No, no," said another monk. "It's Wednesday, I swear."

"It is indeed," someone else declared. "The foxes always bark on a Wednesday."

"They bark when they like," another monk said.

"Thursday it is, when the sun is on the tower."

"Oh no," disagreed a nun in the distance. "Wednesday is today, and the Lady's birthday only a week away now."

"Thursday," someone else insisted. "The birthday is only six days away."

The argument went on and on, with our own heads turning from one to another. By this time there were people insisting it was only Tuesday and others who seemed equally sure it was a Friday today.

At length Aunt Beck said, highly exasperated, "What does it matter what day it is? I only asked to be directed to the king."

"But that is just the point, Wise Woman," said the monk with the green bird. "The King is under geas, poor man. He is forbidden to see strangers on a Thursday."

"Oh," said Aunt Beck. "I've heard tell of this kind of thing in Bernica. What will happen to the king if he does see a stranger on a Thursday?"

"No one knows, except that it's bad to anger the gods," said the little monk. "And—"

"And how do you know I'm a Wise Woman?" Aunt Beck demanded.

"It sticks out a mile," said the monk. "Green Greet saw it at once." He reached up and patted the bird on its head. The bird promptly seized one of his plump little fingers in its beak. I suppose it was meant to be affectionate, but it looked painful. The monk took his hand away and shook it. "Why are you wanting to see the King?" he said. "Are you in need of justice?" He looked from Aunt Beck to me and on to Ogo and Ivar as if the idea puzzled him greatly.

"Not exactly," said Aunt Beck. By this time everyone had stopped arguing and was staring at her with interest. She drew herself up tall. "We are on a mission for the High King of Chaldea," she said.

All the green-robed people seemed impressed by this. Their green hats and little round caps turned and nodded as they looked at one another. "Well, then," said the one with the bird, "it seems best that we take you to our House so that we can divine what day it is.

Would you care to take breakfast with us there?"

"Oh, *yes!*" Ivar said, heartfelt. Ogo's stomach gave a sharp rumble.

"We shall be delighted," said my aunt, stately as ever.

So the group went on choosing fish. I noticed that they did not pay much for it. Most fishermen seemed quite ready to give them fish for nothing. "For luck," said each man, pouring handfuls of tiny silver fish into the baskets.

Beyond the wharf was a market. Here the party acquired armloads of bread, several crocks of butter, a lot of early apples, and a great many cherries. Again, they did not have to pay much for it.

"It's almost worth being holy," Ogo said to me as we went out from the market and among the gray houses of the town. There he nudged me again and pointed. I was just in time to see Plug-Ugly crouched in a patch of sun with a large fish in his mouth. He was gone when we came level with the place. "Do you think that beast is magical?" Ogo whispered.

"Yes," I said. "He must be."

The monks and nuns, chatting cheerfully, led us on to the edge of the town. Their House, when we came to it, was more like a barn than a religious establishment. It was lofty and dark and warm inside, with a fire in the middle of the floor in a most smoky, old-fashioned way. That fire puzzled Ivar because it was low and glowing and made of dark chunks of stuff. Ivar had only seen log fires before. "What are they burning?" he said, peering at it.

"Peat," said Aunt Beck. "This island is made of peat, they say."

Peat seemed to be lumps of marsh, but it served perfectly well to cook fish on. Fishes were sizzling in iron pans in no time. We were each given a heaped wooden plateful of them and nothing but a chunk of bread to eat them with. Everyone sat on the floor to eat. Ogo and Ivar kept getting their long legs in the way. I was as unused as they were to eating on the floor, and I kept having to shift about, trying to get comfortable. Aunt Beck, of course, sat elegantly cross-legged and daintily picked up fish with bread and her fingers as though she had been doing this all her life.

"I call this dreadful!" Ivar grumbled. "It's not *civilized*!" Luckily he had the sense to grumble in a whisper, but even so, Aunt Beck shot him one of her nastiest looks. Ivar turned very red and sat with his back to her after that.

The fish was delicious. We all ate a great deal, being very hungry by then. When we were finished, a grubby rag, which Aunt Beck looked at rather primly, was passed round so we could wipe our fingers. Then the monks and nuns fetched out all manner of strange implements and an abacus and some sheets of parchment and sticks of charcoal and began to calculate which day of the week it actually was.

"I make it Friday," Ogo whispered to me. "We set out on Monday, didn't we?"

Just then the great green bird flew up into the

rafters on a huge spread of green feathers, shouting, "It's Thursday! It's Thursday!"

Ivar and Ogo and I went off into giggles. Aunt Beck said, "I've heard of parrots. It would probably say that if it were Sunday. Quiet now."

But do you know, the monks and nuns *still* couldn't decide what day it was. At last Aunt Beck lost patience and stood up. "We shall go to the king now," she said, "and take a risk on what day it is. Can someone set us on our way, please?"

The monk who owned the parrot stood up too. We had gathered by then that his name was Finn. "I'll take them," he said, "and bring them back if need be. Does anyone know what became of my sandals?"

There was much hunting round the edges of the barn, and a nun eventually produced a pair of thick leather sandals. Finn stamped his chubby feet into them and beckoned the green bird down to his shoulder. "Off we go," he said, cheerfully picking up Aunt Beck's bag. Ogo picked up his and Ivar's, I picked up mine, and we thanked the others and left. As we went, they were busy feeding the animals, almost as if they had forgotten us.

"Is it far to the King? " I asked as we left the houses behind.

"A mile or so," Finn said.

I was glad. My bag was heavy. I envied Ivar striding ahead with Aunt Beck. We were taking a track that led gently upward among dozens of small green fields, most with sheep in them but some growing crops I couldn't recognize. There was honeysuckle in the hedges. The air smelled moist and sweet. Every so often it rained a little—fine rain that made my eyebrows itch and Finn's parrot shake its feathers irritably.

"Bernica is the most western of our islands," Finn explained to me. "And we get all the rain from the ocean beyond."

"Is that what makes everything so green?" I asked.

Finn nodded, pleased. He seemed pleased about most things. "Bernica is the green place," he said, "loved of the Lady."

"And this King we're going to see rules it all?" Ogo was panting. He was finding things heavy too.

"Oh, bless you, no!" Finn told him. "Colm rules only as far as the mountains."

We all looked around for these mountains. Nothing. I was supposing they must be very far away, and Colm's kingdom very big, when Aunt Beck said, "Do you mean those little hills over there?" She pointed to a line of low green bulges a few miles off.

"I do. I was forgetting you come from the jagged island of Skarr," Finn said. "Bernica is a gentle place."

Ogo began to look contemptuous. Ivar laughed. "Those would hardly count as foothills on Skarr," he said. "Have you had your parrot long?"

"I have had Green Greet for twenty years now, ever since old Bryan died," Finn said. "Before that he was bird to Alun and before that to Sythe, but I never knew Sythe, who died before I was born."

"Then he must be ever so old!" I said.

"He is. He has lost count of how old," Finn told me.

About then we came out from among the fields and joined a level grassy road much cut up with wheel and hoof marks. This led across a wide marshy heath full of rattling rushes. I saw herds of donkeys, cows, and pigs and even some horses in the distance. I wondered how anyone knew which belonged to whom, but I didn't wonder too hard because my bag seemed to get heavier and heavier. Just as I was thinking I couldn't carry it a step farther, we arrived at the king's house.

Ivar was not the only one of us who stared at it scornfully. Even Aunt Beck raised her fine eyebrows at the sight of messy walls of mixed mud and stone sheltered by a few miserable trees. The only thing to be said of the place was that it seemed to cover quite a lot of ground. Otherwise, I have seen more impressive farmhouses.

There was a rough wooden door in the messy wall with a fellow standing guard in front of it. He was a fine tall young man with wavy fairish hair and an extremely handsome face. He wore leather armor on his chest and legs with a helmet on his head, and he was armed to the teeth. He had a spear with a wicked sharp point, a sword and a dagger on his great studded belt, and a bow in his hand. A quiver of arrows—also wickedly sharp—hung off his shoulder. I thankfully put down my bag and rubbed my sore hands together while I admired him. He was truly beautiful, except that he was scowling at us.

"What do you want?" he said. "You should know better than to come here on a Thursday."

"So Green Greet was right," Finn murmured. He said to the young man, "These people are a delegation from Skarr, young sir, sent to meet with the King."

"Then they must come back tomorrow," the young man said. "The King's geas forbids him to see strangers on a Thursday."

Finn turned away, looking resigned. "We'll go back to town," he said.

"No, we shall *not!*" Aunt Beck said. "I have not come all this way to be turned back like a nobody. I am

Beck, the Wise Woman of Skarr, and I insist on being allowed to enter!" She drew herself up and looked really formidable.

The sentry drew himself up too. "And I am Shawn, third son of King Colm," he said. "And I refuse to let you enter here."

"*I'm* a king's son too," said Ivar.

"Shut up," said my aunt. "How severe is the geas? How are you so sure it's Thursday? And how do I know your King doesn't just use this excuse to be lazy?"

"It is a strong, strong geas," Shawn retorted. "And kings have a right to be lazy."

"Not when I'm at their gate, they've not!" said my aunt. "Stand aside and let us through this instant!"

"No," said the sentry.

"Very well," said Aunt Beck. She put one hand out to the young man's armored chest and moved him aside. He didn't seem to be able to stop her. He simply stood where Aunt Beck had put him, gaping rather.

I thought and wondered and thought how Aunt

Beck did this, and I still can't see it. I tried to do it myself, experimenting on Ogo and Ivar. Ogo just said, "Why are you pushing me?" and Ivar said, "Who do you think you're shoving?" and neither of them moved. Aunt Beck must have been using some art of the Wise Woman that you only get when you're initiated. And of course I wasn't.

Anyway, the rough wooden door seemed not to have a lock of any kind. Aunt Beck opened it with one bony knee and beckoned us impatiently through. We picked up our bags and trudged through into a small, muddy yard full of ale barrels and on into the king's house itself. The door there was standing open—probably for light, because the hall inside was very dim. There were quite a lot of people inside, all sitting about and yawning. They all jumped and stared at us as Aunt Beck led us in. The green bird on Finn's shoulder squawked out, "It's Thursday, King Colm. It's Thursday."

King Colm was sitting in a big chair at the far end. I think he was asleep until the green bird spoke. He was rather fat, and his belly quivered as he sprang awake and roared out, "What are you doing in here, woman?"

Shawn, the sentry, came rushing in past us. "Forgive me, Father!" he said. "She would come in, whatever I said. I think she's a witch!"

"No, I am not, young man," Aunt Beck retorted. "I am the Wise Woman of Skarr, I'll have you know!"

"I don't care who you are," said the King. "Didn't anyone tell you I am under a geas not to see strangers on a Thursday?"

"Yes, but I've no patience with that nonsense," Aunt Beck said. "What do you imagine will happen now you've set eyes on us?"

"How should I know?" the King said. He looked rather nervously up at the dark beams in the ceiling. "All I know is that the gods will be angry."

Aunt Beck opened her mouth. Almost certainly she was going to say, "Nonsense!" But at that moment there was a tremendous CRASH somewhere outside. People began yelling and screaming out there, hens cackled, pigs squealed, and donkeys brayed. Aunt Beck said, "Well I never!" instead.

King Colm, with his face as well as his belly wobbling, got up and hurried to a door near his chair. Shawn sped after him, crying out, "Father! Be careful!" and Aunt Beck strode after Shawn. Ogo and I looked at each other, dumped our bags, and raced after Aunt Beck.

We came out into quite a big farmyard sort of place. There were sheds and huts all round it, some of which seemed to be for people and some for pigs, hens, or geese. One seemed to be a hay barn. In the middle of the farmyard was a smoking hole. Steam was rising from the mud around it. People—women, children, and old men mostly—were backed against the huts, staring at the hole or—if they were very young— burying their faces in their mothers' skirts and crying. Alarmed hens and indignant goats were running all over the place, while a squad of donkeys crowded into one corner and made the sort of dreadful noise only donkeys can make.

We all hurried to the hole. In fact, we were practically pushed there by all the men crowding out of the hall behind us, Ivar among them. It was a deepish hole. At the bottom of it lay a small black smoking stone.

Aunt Beck said, almost drowned out by the donkeys, "That's a meteorite."

"A fallen star!" the King cried out. "Sent by the gods to punish me!"

"Och, man, don't talk rubbish!" said Aunt Beck. "If the gods aimed it, they missed you."

"I tell you it's my geas!" bawled the King. "My fate!"

I discovered Finn beside me, looking down into the hole, interested. On his shoulder, the green bird was equally interested. It put its head this way, then that, to inspect the smoking stone, and the lines around its eyes looked wiser than ever. "A meteorite, a meteorite," it muttered. Then it stood up tall on Finn's shoulder. "The geas is broken!" it said.

Finn turned his head to look at it. "Are you sure of that?" he demanded.

"Sure of that," the bird echoed.

"Good," said Finn, and reached to tap the King's shoulder. "Majesty," he said loudly, "your geas is broken."

King Colm turned and glared at the little monk. It was fairly plain to me that he had cherished that geas. "And what makes you say that?" he demanded.

"Green Greet says so," Finn explained. "He is a messenger of the gods."

The King stared at the bird. So did Aunt Beck. "That parrot?" she said.

"A messenger of the gods," the parrot said to her.

"You're just repeating what your owner says," my aunt told it, and I confess I would have said the same. Except that no one else had said, "The geas is broken."

"No, I'm not," said the bird. "It's Thursday. The geas is broken. I'm sure of that. It's Thursday."

"A marvel, isn't he?" Finn said, smiling all over his chubby face.

"Hmm," said my aunt. She turned to the King.

"Well, Majesty, it looks as if your lazy Thursdays are at an end."

"By your doing, woman," the King said bitterly. "Why couldn't that bird have just kept quiet?" He sighed, because everyone crowding the farmyard seemed to have heard the bird quite clearly. They were all smiling and thumping one another on the back and congratulating Shawn on his father's delivery. "And why couldn't you have kept the woman *out*?" the king said to his son. "That geas has been handed down, father to son, for hundreds of years. You'll live to regret this."

Shawn looked startled. "I've always thought the geas would go to one of my brothers," he said. "Why me?"

"Because you failed to guard the gate, of course," the King said.

"I fail to see," Aunt Beck said, "why inheriting a nonexistent curse would bother anyone. Majesty, we—"

"Oh, be quiet, woman!" ordered the king. "Who knows what trouble will fill the hole where my geas was, every Thursday. You've brought bad luck to my family. What do I need to do to make you go away?"

Aunt Beck looked decidedly taken aback. Finn said placatingly, "Majesty, they are from the High King of Chaldea, who has sent them on a mission to Bernica."

The King said testily, "No doubt he wanted to get rid of her too. All right, all right. Come back into the hall, woman, and tell me why you've been sent to shake up Bernica. Does he want me to wage war on Gallis, or what?"

I could see Aunt Beck was seething with rage at being treated so disrespectfully. As we all trooped indoors again after the King, she was muttering, "I call this downright ungrateful! For two pins I'd put the geas *back*. *And* I'd make it every day of the week!"

But by the time he was in his chair again and we were all standing in front of him, she had a grip on herself. She explained, perfectly politely, how we had been sent to rescue the High King's son and— possibly—to destroy the barrier too.

King Colm said, "Woman, it's all one to me if you choose to attempt the impossible. What do you expect *me* to do about it?"

"To give us your aid, out of the royal goodness of your heart, Majesty," Aunt Beck replied. "If you could set us on our way by providing a donkey and cart, and maybe some food and a little money, I—"

"Money!" exclaimed the King. "Didn't your High King even give you funds for this mission of yours?"

I thought, Oh, dear, he's stingy as well as eccentric!

Aunt Beck drew herself up proudly and said, as if the admission was dragged out of her, "We were given a purse, Majesty, but it proved to be full of stones."

King Colm seemed astounded. A shocked murmur ran round the hall behind us. "But it is the duty of any king," he said, "to show generosity at all times. Very well, you shall have money. And I can probably spare you a cart and a donkey. Is there anything else?"

"One thing," admitted my aunt. "According to the prophecy, we must have with us one man from each of the islands. Have you a man from Bernica you might spare to go with us?"

I had forgotten that we needed this person. For a moment I was very excited, hoping the king would give us Shawn. He was so good-looking. And indeed the king's eyes did move toward his son. Then Finn piped up. He gave a little cough and announced, "Majesty, I am that man. There is no need for you to deprive yourself of anyone. I and Green Greet have already decided to go with these good people on their mission."

"Speak for yourself, speak for yourself," muttered the parrot.

The King gave a great relieved laugh. "Splendid!" he said. "They will have the gods with them, then. Go with my blessing, Finn Fitzfinn. And be careful," he added to my aunt, "that this monk doesn't eat and drink you out of all my money."

So that was that. Half an hour later we drove out of the king's back gate in a neat little cart, with Aunt Beck driving a neat little donkey with a black line all round her like a tidemark. The people who hitched the donkey to the cart didn't seem to think she had a name, so I called her Moe. I don't know why, except that it suited her. There was food in the cart and jars of ale, and as she drove, my aunt kept smugly patting the fat purse on her belt.

~VII~

The way was very level and green, first through more of the little fields and then through wide-open boglands. Moe trotted cheerfully on, pulling the rattling little cart, while we took turns to ride. There was only room for two of us beside the person driving. I don't think Moe could have pulled all five of us anyway. She certainly couldn't when we came to the hills. There everyone except Aunt Beck had to walk.

But while we were on the levels, Aunt Beck was very talkative. She had a long discussion about religion with Finn, while Ogo sat looking glum and mystified and

Green Greet kept saying, "Mind your own business! Mind your own business!" until, Ogo said later, he wanted to wring the bird's neck. When it was Ivar's turn and mine to ride, Ogo went striding ahead to cool off, and Aunt Beck said to Ivar, "You were mighty slow coming out of the hall when the meteorite fell. What kept you?"

Ivar shrugged. "It sounded dangerous out there."

"It was. Someone could have been injured," Aunt Beck said. "You could have helped them."

"Someone in my position," Ivar said, "being a king's son and all, has to be careful. I could have been killed! I don't think Bernica's gods take much care of people."

"But they do," said my aunt. "That thunderbolt didn't hurt so much as a chicken! What are you being so careful of yourself *for*, may I ask?"

Ivar was surprised she should ask. So was I, as a matter of fact. "I could be King one day," Ivar said. "At the rate my brother carries on, I could be King tomorrow."

"If you think that, you're a greater fool than I took

you for," Aunt Beck snapped. "Your brother Donal is a very canny young man *and* one that lands on his feet like a cat, I may tell you."

"I don't *think* it exactly," Ivar protested.

It seemed to me that Aunt Beck was trying to show Ivar up in the worst possible light. First he was a coward to her and then he was stupidly ambitious. Without waiting for what she might make him out to be next, I interrupted. "Aunt Beck, what made you think of going to King Colm?"

Aunt Beck, as I hoped, was distracted. "It was our obvious choice, Aileen," she told me. "We were in a strange land with no money, no food, no transport, and we had a task to do. All kings are supposed to be generous, provided you can give them a high enough reason. And as you see, it worked, although I must say"—she went on in a most disapproving way—"I'd not expected to find a fat man snoring in a smoky barn and clinging to his geas as an excuse to be lazy. If I were his wife, now—and I think his queen must be as bad as he is—I wouldn't stand for it longer than a week."

And she was off on a tirade about King Colm and his court that lasted until we reached the first of the hills. She seemed to have noticed far more details than I had. She mentioned everything, from the dust on the king's chair to the squalor in the farmyard. I remember her going on about the gravy stains on the king's clothes, the laziness of his household, his underfed pigs, and the ungroomed state of his horses, but I didn't attend very hard. My attention kept being drawn to a softness and a throbbing by my shins. I kept looking down, but there was nothing in the cart but our bags and the food. In the end I reached down and felt at the place. My fingers met whiskers, a cold nose, and a couple of firm upstanding ears on a large round head. It was as I half expected: Plug-Ugly. Invisible. Who would have thought such an ill-looking and magical cat could have such very soft fur? I couldn't resist stroking him—he was like warm velvet—and I could easily do this unnoticed since Ivar was staring moodily over the edge of the cart, highly offended by Aunt Beck's accusations, and Aunt Beck herself was haranguing the landscape.

Actually, Finn was listening to her as he trotted beside the cart. "Hold your horses, Wisdom!" he protested as Aunt Beck moved on to the tumbledown state of the huts in the farmyard. "Why *should* a king be grand? Give me a reason."

"For an example to the rest," my aunt retorted. "For *standards*, of course. And talking of standards . . ." And she was off again, this time about the responsibilities of a king to set an example to his subjects.

Plug-Ugly purred. He rumbled so loudly I was amazed none of the others heard. Or maybe Green Greet did. He interrupted Aunt Beck's discourse by saying, "Claws and teeth, claws and teeth underneath!" but no one took any notice, except my aunt, who turned to the parrot and said, "If that's to my address, shut your beak, my good bird, or you'll be sorry!"

Green Greet rolled his wise eyes around to her and stopped speaking.

The hills, as I said, were hard for Moe the donkey,

and for Finn, who puffed and panted and went pink in the face, but like nothing to the rest of us. Bernica is a low country with lumps in it, and nothing like the deep slopes of Skarr. As Moe toiled up the hill, I looked round at the green, green landscape, dappled with moving patches of sun from among the moist purple clouds, and I thought I had never seen such lovely countryside. It came on to rain near the top of the hill, and at once there was a rainbow arching over it all. I found it glorious.

"Pah!" said Aunt Beck. "Wet."

I could tell she was in a really bad mood. When Aunt Beck gets like that, the safest thing is to keep quiet, but none of the other three seemed to understand this. Finn said soothingly, "Ah, but Wisdom, the rain is what greens our lovely island so."

Aunt Beck made a low, growling noise. She hates being soothed.

Then Ivar asked innocently, "Where are we going? Do you know the way?"

"To the next town, of course!" Aunt Beck

snapped. "Cool Knock, or some such name."

"Coolochie, Wisdom," Finn corrected her.

"And of *course* I know the way!" snarled my aunt. "I was here as a girl, for my sins."

"But—" said Ivar.

Ogo tried to help. "The Prince really means," he said, "what is our route? Don't we have to make for Gallis?"

This got him in trouble from two directions. Ivar said, "Don't speak for me. Dolt!" Aunt Beck glared at Ogo and snapped, "Naturally we do, you great fool! We go southeast, down to the Straits of Charka and find another boat. Do you think I don't know what I'm doing?"

Ivar still didn't seem to understand. "How do we go? Is it very far?" he said.

"Shut up," said my aunt. "You're a fool too!"

Ivar looked so puzzled at this that Finn sidled up to him and whispered, "It will be three or four days for the journey. Bernica is larger than Skarr, but not so large as Logra."

"Did the boy learn no geography?" Aunt Beck asked the wet sky.

After this I cannot remember anyone else speaking much for the rest of the day. We stopped for a silent picnic of bread, ham, and plums and then went on across the green, pillowy plain. By dusk it was raining really hard and quite obvious that we were not going to make Coolochie that day. We were forced to stop at a damp little inn for the night.

Aunt Beck glowered at the rain pattering off its thatch and the green moss growing up its walls. "I *hate* Bernica!" she said.

I sometimes wonder if my story would have been different if the beds in the inn had been comfortable. They were not. The mattresses seemed to have been stuffed with gorse bushes. They prickled and they rustled and the bed frames creaked, and I know it was hours until I got to sleep—and I only slept when Plug-Ugly came creeping in beside me, warm and soft. Aunt Beck probably had a worse night than I did. When I got up soon after cockcrow, she was still fast asleep, looking exhausted. I crept away downstairs, where I found that Ivar had ordered a splendid breakfast for himself and Ogo and Finn but forgotten Aunt Beck and me entirely.

"I'll order more for you now," he said. "Does Beck want any?"

My aunt never eats much for breakfast, but she does like her tea. When I asked in the kitchen, they only had nettle tea. No chamomile, no thyme, no rose hip. I told them to take her up a mug of what they had and went out into the yard to see to Moe. Ogo had made sure she was fed, luckily, *and* brushed her down, and Plug-Ugly was sitting in the cart, fully visible, eating the rest of the ham. I went and sat with him and finished most of the bread and most of the plums.

"You *are* a strange creature," I said to him. "What are you *really*?"

He just rubbed his head against my arm and purred. So we sat happily side by side until an uproar broke out in the inn. I could hear the landlord and his wife protesting mightily, sharp cracks of anger from Aunt Beck, Finn shouting for peace, and Ivar yelling that it was *not his fault*. Shortly both Ogo and Ivar shot into the yard, still eating, and Finn hurried after them, feeding a handful of raisins to Green Greet.

"What *is* going on?" I said.

"Your aunt's being a *sow*!" Ivar said through his mouthful.

"Sure, she meant for us to eat in the cart as we traveled," Finn explained.

It turned out that Aunt Beck had not budgeted for our stay at the inn, or for the breakfasts—Ivar and Ogo had, of course, eaten the food they'd ordered for me. And I and Plug-Ugly had eaten the rest of the food in the cart. Aunt Beck was furious because this meant that we had to buy food in Coolochie now. I must say I didn't feel this was a very good reason for being so angry. I put it down to the bad night on the bad bed, and I sympathized with Ivar when he kept saying, "She could have *told* us!"

We set off under another rainbow—a great double one—as a very subdued group, Aunt Beck all upright, with her mouth pressed into an angry line, and the rest of us hardly daring to say a word. Only Green Greet said anything, and he kept squawking, "Double bow, double measure!" Aunt Beck shot him looks as she drove, as if she was longing to wring his green, feathery neck.

We reached Coolochie around midday. Ivar made moans of disgust when he saw it. It was not a large place, and its walls were made of mud. Inside the big sagging gates, houses were crowded irregularly around a marketplace, and it all smelled, rather.

"I'll say this for Skarr," Ogo murmured to me as the cart squished its way into the market. "At least your towns smell *clean*."

"Of *course* they do," I said proudly. "And I suppose you remember the towns in Logra so well!"

"Not really," he said. "But I do remember there was no mud on the streets."

I sighed. Logra was all perfect in Ogo's memory.

Aunt Beck meanwhile drove the cart among the scattering of poor-looking market stalls and drew up grandly in front of the largest. I looked at its stack of elderly cabbages and the flies hovering round the small heap of bacon and hoped she was not going to buy either of those.

Actually my aunt is a good shopper. She managed to assemble some quite decent provisions and sent Finn off to the bread stall while she bargained for what she had chosen.

"Why are you sending *him*?" Ivar wanted to know.

"He's a monk. He'll get half of it free," my aunt snapped, and turned back to the bargaining.

This did not go well. Whatever price Aunt Beck suggested, the woman behind the stall named a higher one. And when Aunt Beck protested, all the woman would say was "You must remember there's a war on."

"What war is this?" my aunt demanded.

"The war against the Finens, of course," the woman said.

"What are the Finens?" said Aunt Beck.

"Cheating monsters from Ballyhoyle way" was the answer. "You must know that the Finens never paid us for our cloth in my grandmother's time. And were forever cheating and lying ever since. So last month our men went and took their sheep for payment. Last week the Finens came, asking for the sheep back. But naturally we had eaten them by then, so the Finens took all our cattle and the food out of the fields, and when we asked for it back, they threw stones. So yesterday our men took up their weapons and went out to teach the Finens a lesson or two. There was a great battle then."

"Who won?" Ivar asked with interest.

The woman shrugged. "Who knows? For all we can tell, the fighting still goes on."

"But I am sure," Finn said, arriving back with a great basket of bread rolls, "that the might of the men of Coolochie will prevail."

The woman looked pleased at this, but she did not let Aunt Beck have the food any cheaper. Aunt Beck sighed and graciously paid over most of the money King Colm had given her. "And now let's get out of here," she said to the rest of us.

We had lunch a couple of miles on into the plains beyond Coolochie. "Do you think Coolochie's in the right in this war?" Ogo asked, thinking about it as he munched.

"Of course not," Aunt Beck said irritably. "Both sides are complete blackguards. From the sound of it they've been stealing each other's property for centuries. Are you finished? Let's be on our way. I want to be out of this miserable country as soon as I can be."

We had none of us really finished, but no one liked to argue with Aunt Beck in this mood, so we walked along still eating. Finn said soothingly, "You'll find Bernica's not so bad, Wisdom, when you're used to our ways."

Aunt Beck shuddered.

We came over a couple of gentle rises to find the war blocking our road.

The road here divided into several flat green tracks.

Spread out over most of them was a bright-colored struggling mass of people. We could see red, yellow, and orange crests of feathers, shining swords lifting and hacking, and long shields painted with lurid designs. There were yells, hoots, and groans. Every so often a pair of fighters would come loose from the rest and rush across the nearby fields, plunging into ditches and through ponds and screaming insults as they whacked at each other's shields. Meanwhile the battle heaved and walloped away across all the tracks but the one on the extreme left.

Aunt Beck pulled Moe up in disgust. Ivar, rather nervously, half drew his sword. Ogo made as if to pull his dirk out and then thought better of it. There were a lot of people there. Finn made religious signs.

"Do we wait?" I asked Aunt Beck. "They must have been going for a day and a night by now."

"I suppose so," my aunt replied sourly. "They have to stop soon."

"No, no!" squawked Green Greet.

"Oh, no, Wisdom," Finn said. "You see, they will have prayed each man to his chosen god for strength to fight for a week. And poured whisky out to seal the bargain."

"What a waste of good liquor," said my aunt. "But I see that they have."

So did I see, now I thought. There was an invisible cloud hanging over the tussling men that was strong enough to feel. "So what do we do?" I asked.

"We take the only free road," Aunt Beck said, sighing, "and hope that it leads us to a king sometime soon." She clucked to Moe, and we set off again, slowly and cautiously, along the left-hand track. I felt nervous sweat break out all over me as we came closer and closer to the war. I was ready to scream as we came level with it. The red faces, the grunts, and the banging were simply appalling. Once the battle was a little way behind us, it was almost worse. We all went with our heads turned over our right shoulders, in case someone broke away and came after us, and none of us spoke until we had put a low hill between us and the fighting.

Then Finn took off his frayed green cap and mopped his face with it. "Praise the goddess!" he said. Then he laughed. "You spoke of a king, Wisdom," he said, "but in this part of the country we are quite as likely to find a queen. Queens are very frequent here. Does this worry you, Wisdom?"

"Not at all," said my aunt. "Women have far more sense than men."

Ivar snorted at this, but at least he had the sense not to say anything.

We went along the track for some way until, about the time the noise from the fighting died out of hearing, the way suddenly divided into three. Aunt Beck pulled Moe up again.

"Now this is very annoying," she said. "Finn, have you any idea which is our way to go?"

Finn looked absolutely nonplussed. "No, Wisdom. Can you not divine?"

"Oh!" cried my aunt, quite exasperated. "I thought

you were our native guide! Very well. Aileen, unpack my divining bowl from the green bag, will you?"

We moved the cart over beside a convenient flat stone, while I dug in the bag, which still smelled strongly of seawater, and disentangled the bowl from Aunt Beck's underclothes. Everyone gathered round to watch except Ivar, who sat loftily facing the other way, trying not to yawn. Ogo leaned over my shoulder. Green Greet sat on the edge of the cart, bending over to look, with Finn beside him in exactly the same attitude. I felt Plug-Ugly's soft coat brushing my legs as he came to watch too.

"Now—" said my aunt.

She was interrupted by a little red-haired man who had evidently been dozing with his back against the stone. "What's all this?" he said. "Clattering bowls about. Can't a man sleep?"

"I beg your pardon," my aunt said icily. "I was merely trying to divine the right way to go."

"Oh, I can tell you *that*," the man retorted. "No

need at all to clatter. Take the middle way. That will bring you to your queen." And he settled down to sleep again with his pointed chin on his chest.

"Thank you," said Aunt Beck. "I think," she added when the fellow just snored. Nevertheless, she got back into the cart. I put the bowl away again, and we went on down the central road of the three.

Finn and Green Greet seemed mightily disappointed. Finn said, "And here was I hoping to see a Wisdom at work!"

Ivar muttered that he couldn't see what difference it made *which* road we took. "It's all the same in this beastly flat country," he told Ogo.

Ogo said, "Funny, I feel the same way about Skarr."

"What do you mean?" Ivar demanded. "Skarr's not flat."

"No, but there's always just another mountain," Ogo said.

"Oh, you're such a *fool*!" Ivar said, and went stalking angrily ahead along the turfy track.

"Do you mean that?" I asked Ogo. "Can't you really tell one mountain from another?"

"Well, they have different shapes," Ogo conceded, "but they're all high and steep and rocky and—well—the same *colors*."

I supposed he had a point.

After that we trudged along for miles, through several more showers of rain and rainbows as the sun came out again, until I for one was both tired and hungry.

"Hold up," Finn said to me kindly. "Here we come into the town."

"What town?" Ivar said. There was nothing around us except green humps. They were the sort of humps you get when people have been mining years ago and then gone away and let grass grow over the spoil heaps. These heaps grew taller and taller as we went along. Aunt Beck gave Finn an irritable, puzzled look. "This doesn't look like any town I know."

Finn beamed. He almost glowed, he was so happy.

On his shoulder Green Greet stretched his neck and gave out a most unparrotlike warbling sound. But I had been thinking for some time now that Green Greet was not exactly a parrot. He was more something along the lines of Plug-Ugly, really. Finn lifted his beaming face up to my aunt and said, "No more *should* you know, Wisdom. This is my Lady's town."

I saw what he meant. If I screwed my eyes up and sort of peered at the green humps, I saw them as house-shaped, with green, thatched roofs and high arched doorways. At length Aunt Beck was driving Moe down a wide turf avenue with mansion-sized green houses on either side and ahead a tall, tall hill that managed to be both rounded and castle-shaped at once. She looked down at Finn, trotting beside the cart. "Would you say," she asked, "that the person beside that stone happened to be a leprechaun?"

"Oh certainly, Wisdom," he said joyfully. "No doubt of it."

"Then are we to be wary of tricks?" asked my aunt.

"Only if you invite them, Wisdom," Finn said.

"Hmm," she said.

We reached the castle mound then, and we were suddenly surrounded by little red-haired men, who flooded in from nowhere and took hold of Moe and unhitched her from the cart, chattering all the time.

"Sure, the Queen will be glad of this!" I heard, and, "This is royal visiting! Has no one yet sounded a fanfare?" and "Can you smell the sea on them? They come from distant islands, all but one," and all sorts of other things. "See the bird!"

In no time at all, Moe had been led off one way and the cart hauled away in another and we ourselves ushered into the castle mound. There were different people in there, though they were very hard to see. It was as if there was a veil over everything inside. But if I screwed my eyes up and peered hard, I could tell they were very tall and dressed most magnificently. Almost equally hard to see was the table they led us up to, all laid out with steaming dishes of food, piles of fruit, and golden candlesticks.

"Be pleased to sit and eat," they told us.

Ivar and Ogo made a dive for the tall chairs at the table. Aunt Beck stopped me and looked at Finn with her head on one side, questioningly. "Ought we?"

"You come in friendship. Yes," he said.

So we sat down to eat. It was all delicious, and I saw that there was even a cup of nuts and diced fruit for Green Greet. Dimly on the floor I could see that there were dishes of food for Plug-Ugly. They knew he was there, even if he was invisible. We all had the best meal I'd seen since we left Skarr.

When we had finished, the tall people led us off again, to a place that I knew at once was the throne room. Ogo had eaten so much that he was quietly letting his belt out as we were led in, and he had to stop in embarrassment. The place was one where you had to behave reverently. The air of it was warm, and fresh and cool at the same time, and it was scented like a garden. There were nets in there, though I couldn't see them clearly, with birds in them flitting. Green Greet took off from Finn's shoulder in a whirring of wings and went to perch on one of the half-seen branches.

Then the Queen came forward to greet us. I gasped, she was so beautiful. And merrily and eagerly friendly with it. She wore a green dress that hugged her shape and flared at her feet, with a gold girdle hanging on her hips. I remember thinking, This is how a queen should be! as she came toward us.

"Welcome," she said, and she smiled, meaning the welcome. "It's not often that we see people from Skarr. What brings you to Bernica?"

My aunt stepped forward, very straight and precise. I could see she was still struggling with her bad mood, but she bowed politely and said, "We have been sent on a mission to rescue the High King's son from Haranded, Your Majesty."

"Oh yes, the prophecy," the Queen said, "to raise the barrier too, is it not?" She looked at us all, one by one. "That means you must bring one man from each of the islands. You"—she looked at Ivar—"must be the man from Skarr."

Ivar nodded. "Yes, I'm the son of King Kenig . . ." he agreed, and tipped his head back proudly.

"A Prince, no less," said the Queen, and there was just a trace of mockery in the way she said it. It made me want to jump forward and explain that Ivar had been brought up to be proud of his birth, but I said nothing, because the Queen had turned to Finn by then. Finn, to my surprise, was on both knees and seemed almost terrified. "And you are the man from Bernica?" the Queen said.

Finn clasped both plump hands in front of him as if he were saying his prayers. "Oh, yes, Lady," he more or less whispered, "unless you think me unworthy."

The Queen laughed. "How could I think you unworthy, keeper of Green Greet?" she said.

"Well, sure he does me great honor accepting my care," Finn said.

The Queen glanced up at Green Greet where he

sat among the hard-to-see leaves above us. "What do you say to that, Green Greet?" she asked the bird.

Green Greet put his head to one side and nibbled with his beak. "Honest man," he said. "Man of peace."

"There you have it!" the Queen said, laughing again. She added to Aunt Beck, "You'll have to leave any fighting to these lads, you know!" She looked at Ogo then. "And you, young man?"

Ogo had been staring at her as if she were the most marvelous thing he had ever seen—and I don't blame him: she was truly lovely. When she spoke to him, he blushed bright brick color and went down on one knee. "I—I'm from H-Haranded really," he stammered. "I was brought along as Ivar's servant."

"But rightly brought along," the Queen said. "The prophecy asks for a man from *each* island, doesn't it? And we are four islands. I'm sure you'll prove your worth." She turned to Aunt Beck again. "You'll need your man from Gallis too, of course. I'll give you money to see you there—"

Here, while Aunt Beck was graciously bowing her head in thanks and Ogo was struggling to his feet, looking stunned, the Queen was interrupted by a solid invisible presence that pushed itself up against her skirts. I could clearly see the shape of him in the bellying and rippling of the green fabric.

"Oh, Plug-Ugly!" I said. "Honestly!"

The Queen stooped to put her hand where Plug-Ugly's head seemed to be. "Is that what you call him?" she said. "How did he find you?"

"He was on an island that seemed to be part of Lone, Majesty," I said. "He—er—sort of followed us."

"Or followed you," the Queen said. She turned to Aunt Beck again. "You are very lucky to have such a gifted assistant," she said.

I knew I was blushing redder than Ogo. Aunt Beck shot me a scathing look and answered in her driest way, "If gifted means secretly adopting a stray cat, then I suppose I am lucky, yes."

This did not please the Queen at all. Her beautiful

eyes narrowed, and she said, quite fiercely, "I *know* this cat. He would only follow someone of great abilities."

Aunt Beck shrugged. "I've no idea *what* Aileen's abilities might be."

"My good woman!" the Queen exclaimed. "Why not?"

If there is one thing my aunt hates, it is being called a good woman. She drew herself in like a poker. "Why?" she said. "What a stupid question. Because Aileen failed her initiation, of course."

I think I went even redder. My face was so hot that when I put up my hands to hide it, my fingers were wet with sweat. I *know* Aunt Beck was in a bad mood, but did she *have* to tell the Queen that? I could hear Ivar trying not to laugh.

The Queen made me feel no better by saying angrily, "She can have done no such thing! You must be very unobservant. I can *see* she is as well qualified as you are. And I do not like your manner, woman. I have said I will grant you money, and so I will, but I shall do nothing more to further your mission. And you, particularly, may leave my presence unblessed! Go!" She flung out an arm, pointing.

And that is the last I remember of her. Ogo says he thinks he remembers that people took us and hustled us out of the place. But I only remember being outside, among the green mounds, with Moe already harnessed to the cart beside us. My aunt was clutching a chinking leather bag and looking surprised and angry about it.

Finn was crying, with big tears rolling into his strange beard. "Oh, Wisdom!" he sobbed. "How could you so insult the Lady?"

Green Greet added to this by swirling down from somewhere, crying out, "Unwise Wisdom, unwise Wisdom!"

"Huh!" said Aunt Beck, and stomped her way up into the driving seat, red heels flashing annoyance at us all.

~VIII~

Strange to say, our journey after that did not go well. For one thing, it rained all the rest of the time we were on Bernica. Ivar did not help matters by saying morosely, several times a day, that my aunt should know better than to go around insulting queens. This kept Aunt Beck's bad mood simmering, so that Ogo and Finn hardly dared go near her.

I had to be near her, though, because we shared a damp bed in every damp inn we came to. That first night Aunt Beck took me severely to task about my wretched initiation. "You told me nothing happened that night, Aileen. Why did you lie to me?"

"I *didn't* lie," I wailed. "Nothing happened. I just didn't have any visions, that's all."

"Something *must* have happened," Aunt Beck insisted. "What are you hiding?"

"Nothing," I said. "I *told* you!"

"Nonsense. Tell me about every minute of the time you were in there," my aunt commanded. "Every tiny thing. Out with it."

"You mean," I said, "I have to keep saying, 'I sat there, Aunt Beck, and I shivered, and the floor was cold and hard, Aunt Beck, and it was too dark to see anything, Aunt Beck,' over and over for however many hours I was in there? Because that was what it was like."

"Not all the time," said my aunt. "You were asleep when I hauled the stone back. Did you not dream?"

"Not that I remember," I said, hoping she would stop.

Not she. "So there was no time when you were able

to see even a flicker of light?" she persisted. "Don't shake your head, Aileen. Don't lie."

She went on like this remorselessly, until at last I said, "Well, if you must know, I did see the moon shining in."

"That has to be nonsense," my aunt replied. "The stone was tight to the turf."

"No, it wasn't," I said. "There was a gap, and so I rolled the stone aside and came out for a bit. There!"

"That stone," my aunt said, "had not moved since I rolled it there the night before. I know because I put in two tufts of heather, as we always do, and they were still there in the morning, in the very same places. Or did you think you put them back from the inside through two feet of granite somehow?"

"Oh," I said. "No. I didn't know they were there. I just rocked the stone, and it came out."

"*Did* you?" she said. "And what did you think you saw outside?"

"I didn't *think* I saw, I *saw*!" I said. "It was

everything, just as usual, except the moon made it look as if there had been a frost. I saw our cabin and the hills and the sea and the full moon—"

"And was there a light in the cabin?" she asked.

I shook my head. "No, it was all dark."

"There should have been a light," Aunt Beck said. "I was keeping vigil for you. You silly child! You go and have a vision and then pretend you didn't!"

"It didn't *feel* like a vision," I mumbled. I felt very foolish. "If it was one, what does it mean?"

"I have no idea," my aunt said, to my great disappointment. "But no wonder that disagreeable Queen thought you were qualified. You clearly are."

"But I don't feel any different," I protested.

"Neither did I," said Aunt Beck. "The powers have been in you all along, so naturally you feel the same."

I said, "I thought I would feel a fizz in my fingers— or at least be able to see into minds."

"Or through walls, maybe?" Aunt Beck said. "Lie down now and get some sleep and don't be so foolish."

I did lie down, but I don't think I would have gone to sleep if Plug-Ugly had not arrived, silent and heavy, to lie across my feet, making that chilly inn bed warm as warm. I was still feeling foolish in the morning, and for several days after that. How was I to know that it had been a vision? I'd never had a vision before. It had all looked so *real*. And it seemed unfair of Aunt Beck to blame *me* because *she* got angry with the Queen.

I gloomed about this as we trudged through rain across soggy green moors for the next few days. Ogo asked me what was wrong. I told him, expecting him to tell me not to be so foolish, like Aunt Beck had. Instead he said, "Er—Aileen, aren't you supposed to be secret about your initiation rites?"

"I don't think so," I said. "It's no great thing, after all."

"Oh," he said. "I remember my uncle saying he was not to say a word about his initiation. He seemed to think it was awfully holy."

"He must have had different rites," I said. "And I do

think Aunt Beck is being unreasonable, blaming me. After all, she was the one who was rude to the Queen."

Ogo looked up at Aunt Beck's proud profile above us in the cart. "She doesn't like Bernica," he said. "She'd have blamed you for *something*."

This was probably true. It was quite comforting.

The next day when we stopped for lunch we were mobbed by donkeys. The inn we stayed at the night before had sold Aunt Beck two loaves and a bag of hard-boiled eggs. My aunt sat on the tailgate of the cart and made sandwiches for us all, with a pot of relish left over from the inn before that. Don't ask me why donkeys should like egg sandwiches. Moe didn't. I offered her some of mine after I'd given some to Plug-Ugly, and she simply plunged her nose back into her nose bag. Green Greet didn't care for them either. But those donkeys must have caught the scent from a mile away. They came thundering in across the wet moor, a whole herd of them, and tried to eat the sandwiches out of our hands. We slapped their noses aside, but it did not deter them. They were wild, hungry donkeys. Some of them had been out on the moor for so long that their front hooves had grown into long, up-curving spikes, like Gallis's slippers. And the ones who got to us first were so determined not to let the latecomers get any of our food that they kept backing round and kicking the slow ones in the ribs. Boom. Like a drum. We were in a savage kicking mob in seconds.

Finn went under the cart and crouched there. Ivar took his sword off his belt, scabbard and all, and hit out at donkeys with it. Slap. Whap. They took no more notice of it than they did of the heels of their own kind. One donkey bit him, and he yelled. Aunt Beck scrambled for her whip, into the cart. I hastily bundled up the rest of the eggs and the bread in the cloths and then had a tug-o'-war for it with a villainous black donkey that saw what I was doing. Ogo was jostled right out beyond the milling herd, where he ran in a half circle, roaring with anger. He found a whippy stick out there and ran in again, bashing at ears and sides. But it was Plug-Ugly who drove the brutes off. I saw him in glimpses, leaping from donkey to donkey, raking with his claws at every one. You could not believe the yelling and braying that made. At length Aunt Beck snatched Moe's meal off her and drove her away down the track at a gallop. Moe was only too glad to go. The rest of us ran after her. The last I saw of the donkeys, they were in a fleeing gray huddle with Plug-Ugly bounding after them.

Ogo and Ivar thought it was ever so funny. When we finally stopped for lunch a second time, in a glen halfway up one of the low hills, they kept saying, "An attack by robbers!" Then they roared with laughter.

"Lucky it was," said Finn, "that the robbers were not human."

"Are there many robbers in these parts?" my aunt asked sharply.

"I have never been in these parts, Wisdom. I don't know," Finn said.

This made me feel quite nervous. But the boys

continued to make jokes about the brave way we had beaten off the band of robbers.

"It wasn't you; it was Plug-Ugly," I said to Ogo while we packed up to go on.

"We all combined," he said merrily. "A great combat."

Plug-Ugly seemed to turn up again while we were making our way down the other side of the little mountains. I felt him brush against my legs as I walked. Green Greet could see him. I saw him swivel his head to look down at the place where Plug-Ugly was, and I wondered at the strangeness of both creatures.

As the track curved, we had a dim, rainy view of more small fields below. It looked as if we were coming to another kingdom of some kind. But it was all misty, until the clouds parted just a little to let through one bright shaft of sunlight. The brightness traveled across fields and some houses, and swept on up and across us. For a moment we walked in bright greenness, and I distinctly saw the gaunt shadow of Plug-Ugly trotting beside mine, before the sunlight swept on, over the hill and away.

"Hmm," said Aunt Beck, watching it travel. "I'm not sure I like that."

We went on to the next bend in the track, where we were suddenly surrounded by armed men. They seemed to come out of the rain from nowhere, all in black, with black beards and grim faces, and all with swords drawn or spears poised.

"Oo-er," said Ogo. "Real robbers."

My aunt stopped the cart and looked at them. "And what do you gentlemen want?" she said. "I assure you we have very little worth taking."

The nearest and grimmest man said, "You're all under arrest. The Queen's orders."

And they wouldn't say anything more. They just crowded in around us, smelling of sweat and wet leather, and marched us on down. The only thing they said, when I asked, "Who is the Queen here, then?" was to answer, "The Lady Loma, of course. Hold your tongue."

Down we went, quite quickly, and very soon came into a wide yard inside a tall stockade. In the usual manner of Bernica, there were pigs everywhere, and some cows, and chickens too, but all silent and ominous. There were a whole lot more men here, and women too, who came to stand in a ring around us, arms folded, looking most unfriendly. The grim men made us get away from the cart and wait there in the rain while they scrambled into the cart and proceeded to go through our baggage. We had to watch them heave out all our clothes into the wet and then shake out our bags, then go through the remains of the eggs and the bread. They took a large cheese I didn't know we had but left the rest.

"This," said my aunt, "is an outrage. What are they looking for?"

Whatever it was, they didn't find it. They helped themselves to Ivar's best cloak and my nice dress and Aunt Beck's spare plaid, but they stopped when a murmur began in the watching ring of people. Some were saying, "Here they come," and others were whispering, "Here's the Lady Loma now." The cheese and the garments were promptly passed from hand to hand and vanished as the queen arrived.

She was a mighty figure. I had never seen a woman so tall and so fat. She was all in red, a huge garment like a tent, that clashed with the mauve-red of her face and the ginger of her hair. And she was drunk. We could smell whisky from where we stood, and the several smaller women with her kept having to push her upright as she swayed this way and that until she fetched up against the cart with a thump. There she stood, squinting and glowering at us.

"Mercy!" I heard Finn say. "It's the Red Woman herself!"

"What," said Aunt Beck, "is the meaning of this, Your Majesty? I'll have you know I'm the Wise Woman of Skarr, here on legal business for the High King, and I can't be doing with this sort of thing."

The Lady Loma answered, in a great slurred voice,

"Hold your tongue, woman! You're on trial for injuring my donkeysh, so you are. Here they come. Shee. Look!"

And in through the stockade gate came trotting the whole herd of those wild donkeys, roped head to tail and led by a couple more of the grim men. There was no doubt they were the same ones that had mobbed our cart. I recognized the wicked black donkey with the up-curved hooves, second in the line. And I saw that it, and most of the others, had Plug-Ugly's bleeding claw marks on its unkempt rump. Oh dear, I thought.

Ogo, who had rounded up more than his fair share of donkeys in his time, muttered, "How did they get them here so *quick*?"

A good question. And as the donkeys were driven up beside us, stinking and steaming, I was afraid I knew the answer. The Lady Loma seemed to cast a shadow across the beasts as they came near her, and that shadow showed another shadow inside each donkey, a shadow bent and skinny, with only two legs. I was pretty sure those donkeys had once been men and women. And I was very frightened indeed. I just hoped my aunt would be a bit more polite when she saw the shadows too.

But Aunt Beck didn't seem to notice. She stared haughtily at the drunken queen. "So?" she said. "These beasts of yours attacked our cart for food. Do you blame us for beating them off?"

"I shurely do," growled the Lady Loma. "Jusht look at the blood on my poor dumb beashtsh! You'd no call to hurt them sho! I blame you for that, woman!"

"They wouldn't have gone otherwise," retorted my aunt. "And if we're to talk of blame, Your Majesty, who was it turned this herd out to starve on moss and small grasses? Who was it left their hooves in that state? Who was it never gave any care to their hides or their teeth or their health generally? I'll tell you straight, Majesty, that herd is a *disgrace* to its owner!"

"It is not sho!" growled the Queen. "It ish a proud band, sho it ish."

The two glared at each other. I could see what my aunt was trying to do. She was trying to impress the

Lady Loma with her personality, the way she usually did others. But I was fairly sure it was not going to work, not when the lady was clearly a powerful witch, and drunk besides. I could hear Finn whispering, "Oh, *don't*, Wisdom! Don't!" I could feel Plug-Ugly pressing himself invisibly against my legs, and I didn't wonder that he was frightened too—except that he wasn't frightened, really. He was trying to comfort me because he knew how scared I was.

"It is *not* proud," said my aunt. "It's one of the sorriest I ever saw. But if it makes you feel better, I apologize for any damage to your herd. What recompense do you want?"

"Recompenshe!" howled the Queen, swaying about so that our cart creaked and poor Moe turned her head and waggled her ears, looking most uncomfortable. "*Recompenshe?* I tell you, woman, there is only one recompenshe you can make. Itsh *thish!*" And she lunged forward, pointing at Aunt Beck with one great mauve hand and making wild gestures with the other.

I was fairly sure she meant Aunt Beck to turn into a

donkey too. But it didn't work. Maybe it was because my aunt's personality was too strong, or maybe it was because the Lady Loma nearly overbalanced with the violence of her gestures and the women with her had to haul her upright again. What did happen, though, was almost as alarming. Aunt Beck's proud face went pale and slack. Her mouth hung open, and her knees gave way. Ivar and I managed to catch her before she quite fell down, and we held her up, facing the Queen. Ivar had a sickly, placating smile. I don't know how I looked—accusing, I think. I saw Finn was on his knees and Ogo was bowing with his hands together like a person praying.

The Lady Loma stared, squinting at us all. Then she grunted, "What a showy band indeed. Get them out of my shight," and staggered away from the cart to go back to the big building across the yard.

"Will we keep their cart, Lady?" one of the men called after her.

We'd have lost the cart then, as well as Aunt Beck's wits, if Green Greet had not taken a hand. He flew into the air in a great green whirl and stayed there, flapping in front of the Lady Loma's face. "Remember the curse!" he shrieked. "Remember the curse!"

The Lady Loma put up one thick arm to shield her face and shouted, "And curse you too, you feshtering bird!" Then she yelled over her shoulder, "Jusht turn them out, cart and all!" After that she went staggering away among the hens and pigs, bawling to her women, "Am I Queen here or am I not? What right hash that bird? What *right*?"

Green Greet came flapping back to perch on the cart, satisfied. The grim men and the other people began hastily throwing our things back into the cart—minus the garments and the cheese, though—while Finn trotted to Moe's head to turn her around and, in the distance, the women made soothing noises at the yelling queen. It was easy to see that everyone was scared stiff of her. Fair enough, if she turned someone into a donkey every time she was annoyed. I was pretty scared myself. I didn't breathe easy until I had coaxed Aunt Beck to sit in the cart and Ivar had driven it out of the stockade.

~IX~

I had to explain to everyone what had happened, once we were back on the track. At least Finn seemed to know. Apparently the Red Woman was famous in Bernica. Finn kept interrupting my explanation with devout cries of "It's lucky we were to come off so easy, bless the Goddess!" But the boys could not seem to understand. Ivar wondered why one of the grim men had not long since run the Lady Loma through when her back was turned.

Ogo said thoughtfully, "Better to put a pillow over her face while she was asleep and then sit on it."

This surprised me coming from Ogo, but I said patiently, "No, you'd both be donkeys in an instant if you tried either of those things. She's *powerful*. She'd know. She'd see your intention before you started."

"You mean," Ivar said incredulously, "that great cow of a woman can actually turn *people* into *donkeys*?"

"Indeed she can," said Finn. "And does."

"While she's that drunk?" said Ivar.

"Yes," I said. "She probably does it oftener when she's drunk."

"And she's seldom sober, they say," Finn added.

"But," Ogo pointed out, "she didn't turn Beck into a donkey, did she?"

"She tried," I said.

"I could see she tried something," Ogo admitted.

"They'd got themselves a neat setup there," Ivar said cynically—and typically. "They set the herd on travelers, then arrest them, and then take all their property, but it's hard to see it as witchcraft. My brother would appreciate that trick."

"*Why* didn't your aunt get turned into a donkey?" Ogo persisted.

"She's too strong-minded," I said. "I think."

"She is that," Finn agreed. "She'll be coming to herself anytime soon now."

We all looked at Aunt Beck sitting upright and empty-faced among the baggage, all of us sure that Finn was right and that Aunt Beck would rise up any moment and take over the driving from Ivar.

She didn't.

When it came near evening, Aunt Beck was still sitting there. If we spoke to her, she would only answer if we said it several times, and then it was "Don't know, I'm sure," in the vaguest voice. It was alarming.

Meanwhile, we had passed over some more low hills to where the country felt different. The green seemed a deeper green, but perhaps this was just because the rain was falling harder. When we came to a small village, Finn scuttled across to a woman who was taking a bucket to the well.

"Tell me, does the Lady Loma rule in this country?" he asked her.

"No, thank the Goddess" was the reply. "These parts belong to Queen Maura."

We all sighed with relief. I think even Moe did. From here on we were all expecting Aunt Beck to begin coming to herself. She didn't. She sat there. I began to feel seriously alarmed. The trouble was, Aunt Beck had of course had charge of the money. But it seemed to be nowhere in the cart. As far as I *knew*, none of the Lady Loma's grim people had found it, but I was not sure. I asked the others if they had seen anyone secretly taking it while we stood inside that stockade. They all thought not.

"I was watching like a hawk," Ivar said. "I even know where they took my cloak. I *know* I'd have seen someone with that money bag. It was quite big."

"Sure, your aunt will have hidden it," Finn said.

"Yes, but *where*?" I said. With evening coming on, we needed to stay at an inn and find somewhere to eat, but we couldn't unless we had money.

"Perhaps it was inside that cheese," Ogo suggested. I wanted to hit him.

We all tried asking Aunt Beck where the money was, but all she would say was that vague "Don't know, I'm sure." It was maddening.

At sunset I lost my temper. There was a good-looking inn just up the road, and we couldn't even buy a bread roll there. By this time I had asked Aunt Beck politely, and kindly, and loudly, and softly, and just asked. I had cajoled. Ogo had pleaded. Finn had prayed to her. Ivar had commanded her to tell him. Then he had shouted. Ogo had tried putting his mouth near her ear and whispering. None of it worked. I made Ivar pull Moe up. I stamped my foot on the stony street. "Beck," I said sharply, "tell me where you hid the money or I'll pull your hair down!"

I must have sounded like my mother, her sister, and she'd gone back to her childhood in a sort of way. She looked up and said, "It's in the beast's food, of course. And if you pull my hair, I'll tell Gran." Their grandmother brought them up, Beck and my mother, you see.

The boys fell on Moe's sack of oats and began plunging their hands into it as if it were a lucky dip. Before they could spill it all, I grabbed up the nose bag, just in case. And it was far heavier than it should have been. Aunt Beck had stowed the purse cunningly near the top so that it would not show as a bulge. Poor Moe had been having to eat around it. I pulled it out in triumph. "Here it is!"

We were able to stay at the inn after all. But we discovered that, in order to get my aunt to eat, or to wash, or to get into bed, I had to speak like a cross sister to her. "Beck, eat your supper or I'll tell Gran!" I snapped. Then, later: "Beck, get ready for bed this instant!" And finally: "Beck, lie down and go to sleep, unless you want your hair pulled!"

By then I was sick of snapping. I did so hope she would wake up as her grown-up self in the morning.

She didn't.

I had to begin snapping all over again. "Beck, take your nightgown off. Beck, get your stockings on or there'll be trouble! Get to the outhouse, Beck, before you wet yourself! Eat that porridge, Beck! Beck, get up in the cart or I'll spank you!"

Finn and the boys watched and listened, mouths open sadly. "What a comedown for a great Wisdom," Finn said, shaking his head.

This was all the three of them could think of. It was me who had to pay our shot, and it was me who remembered to ask the road to the Straits of Charka, but at least one of us did.

The Straits, they told me, were southeast of there. Take the left turn at the big crossroads, they told me, and make for the town of Charkpool, where the ferry was. While they talked, I thought of the map our Dominie was always drawing of the islands, with fat Bernica straight up and down and Gallis a long, thin island slanting away from it south and east. And I realized we probably had not far to go. I thanked the inn people very politely and went out to where Ogo was busy harnessing Moe to the cart. Aunt Beck was sitting on a stone, while Ivar marched up and down in front of her. We were all afraid that she might take it into her head to wander off. Finn stood anxiously behind her.

"Good news," I told them. "It sounds as if it's not far to Charkpool."

"And what do we do when we get to Charkpool?" Ivar demanded.

"Get on the ferry to Gallis," I said. "The Straits are not wide." And I hoped that as soon as we set foot on another land, the Lady Loma's spell would be lifted from Aunt Beck. Some magics are like that.

"But isn't Charkpool a port?" Ivar said. "We could get a boat to Skarr there, couldn't we? I don't think we're doing any good with Beck like this. I think we should go home."

I think we all gasped. I felt as if Ivar had given the side of my head a great blow. Home! I thought. Skarr! And I so longed to go home that I *ached*. I wanted the smells and the food and the mountains and *safety*. Somewhere where I knew how the magics worked and where there were proper kings and Wise Women were respected. I wanted it all so much that I nearly cried.

Finn, looking utterly dismayed, said, "But, young Prince, are we not on a mission?"

Ogo seemed appalled. "Give up, you mean?" he said. "We're not even halfway yet."

As he said this, I felt Plug-Ugly come violently up against my legs. I almost fell over.

"Yes," said Ivar. "I think we should give up and go home. We're not likely to get anywhere without a Wise Woman to guide us. Don't look like that, Ogo. You just want to get back to Logra if you can. And you can't."

"I didn't *mean* that!" Ogo said. "And what would become of Finn if we all get on a boat bound for Skarr?"

"Oh, I shan't suffer," Finn assured him. "There are monasteries all over, and all would be honored to house Green Greet. No worry, young sir."

Meanwhile, I was feeling as if Plug-Ugly had given me

a jolt in the opposite direction to Ivar's. For the first time, I really put together the things that had happened before we reached Bernica: the way we had been sent so secretly with a bag of stones instead of money; the way Seamus Hamish had nearly left us on the islet where we found Plug-Ugly and the way he had frankly told us he would be rewarded for coming home without us; and—if I started thinking honestly—the way Ivar's own mother seemed to have tried to poison him, let alone the way she had tried to bewitch Aunt Beck and me. And it all added up to the fact that we were not expected to return to Skarr. In fact, if we *did* return, Skarr would *not* be a place of safety. Far from it. I could not see *why*, but I could see that.

"My father will look after Beck," Ivar was saying. "It makes *sense*, don't you see, to go home now we have no Wise Woman—"

"Ivar," I said, "stop talking nonsense. *I* am a Wise Woman, and of *course* we are going on."

"You?" Ivar said, laughing. "You're only a child! A fat lot of guiding *you* can do! I tell you and I'm a Prince and I'm in charge now—we are going home to Skarr."

"And you'll admit you've failed?" I said, trying to touch the pride I knew he had.

"I was tricked into coming on this stupid mission," he retorted. "There's no shame in admitting failure after that."

"Well, I *would* be ashamed," I shot back. "Of all the cowardly—"

"Oh, peace, peace!" Finn said, wringing his hands. Green Greet was on tiptoes on his shoulder, opening and shutting his wings.

"I tell you what," Ogo put in, "why don't we consult Green Greet?"

This struck me as a strange but clever idea. But Ivar snorted. "Consult a *parrot*?" he said. "Isn't that just typical of you, Ogo."

"He is not a parrot!" Finn said scandalized. "How can you think so when he is known all over Bernica for a wise oracle!"

"Wise oracle, is he?" Ivar said unpleasantly. "All

I've ever heard him do is to echo the last words anyone says. Listen. I'll show you." He swung round Aunt Beck and stood in front of Finn and the green bird on his shoulder. "What say, Green Greet?" he asked. "Do we go home to Skarr? Home to Skarr, home to Skarr?"

Green Greet tipped his head sideways and stared at Ivar out of one round eye. "No," he said very clearly and distinctly. "Go to Gallis, go to Gallis, go to Gallis." It was almost as if he were making fun of Ivar, I swear it.

Ivar went quite pale with astonishment. I said quickly, "That settles it, then. Ogo and Finn and I will go on anyway. If you want to get on a boat for Skarr in Charkpool, Ivar, you can, but you'll have to work your passage because I don't think we've enough money for a fare."

I felt great relief to say this, but scared too. The responsibility of getting us all to Gallis was heavy upon me as we set off, with Aunt Beck sitting in the cart with Finn to mind her and Ogo driving. Ivar refused to drive. He stalked behind, muttering. I walked next to Ogo, trying to chat cheerfully. It was one of those times when I wished I had never fixed on Ivar for my chosen mate. But I didn't feel I could go back on my word to myself, so I put it out of my mind and thought instead how lucky we were to have escaped the dangers of Skarr, whatever they were.

It rained, of course. But it rained in short showers and the sun shone between. That day we saw more rainbows than I had seen in my life up to then. They looked truly lovely over the deep green of Bernica. One—a great double rainbow—made both Ogo and me exclaim. Two great misty colored arches. Then we exclaimed again as a third rainbow shone gently into being inside the other two.

"I've never seen that before," Ogo said.

"That is a promise from the gods," Finn told us as all three rainbows faded away.

"Promises, promises!" Ivar muttered sourly from behind.

I'd hoped the promise was that we'd reach the coast soon, but it was not so. The land went on and on after we had taken the left-hand way at the crossroads, and we had to stay at an inn again that night. Or we tried to. For some reason it was very crowded, so they directed us to a house in the village, where we spent the night next door to a herd of cows. It was very restless. Aunt Beck would hardly do a thing I told her, and I grew sick of snapping at her. But the food was good. We set off in quite good spirits into next day's rain, and when the clouds cleared, we saw the sea again at last, just briefly, between two low hills.

We discovered then why the inn had been so crowded. People came pouring past us, faster than Moe could go, all of them in holiday clothes. The women had layers of different colored petticoats and skirts hitched up with ribbons to show them off. The men had ribbons everywhere and hats with feathers. Most of them called out to us cheerfully, "Going to the Fair, are you?" or "Bound for Charkpool Fair, then?"

When *I* answered, I said, "Maybe." Finn said nothing. But Ivar and Ogo both called back joyfully that of course they were going. At which I sighed and looked around at us all. None of us looked like people on holiday. Aunt Beck was draggled and sagging, nothing like her usual neat self. I had made a mess of helping her do her hair that morning, and she was wisps all over. Goodness knows how my hair looked, but my dress was grubby. Ogo's fine new clothes had become worn old clothes. Ivar was mud to the waist from kicking along behind the cart. Even Finn's ragged green robes were the worse for wear. Ah well, I thought. No one can travel as we had done and stay new and tidy. But it made me very self-conscious.

The road took us round a hill, and there was the Fair in front of us in a wide green meadow, with the town beyond that. And beyond that I could actually see Gallis as woods and mountains, blue with distance. Then I could think of practically nothing else but that there, quite near, was my father's birthplace, as beautiful as he always said it was. I could hardly be bothered with the Fair.

And that was silly because it looked fun. There was a mass of colored tents and a mass of animals and an even greater crowd of people. On the grass in front of me they were dancing to a band of fiddlers. The tunes were fast and jolly and never seemed to end. People dropped out of the dance, panting and laughing, when they had had enough, threw coins into the hats the fiddlers had out in front of them, and then went to the nearest tent for drinks. As for the fiddlers, they played on and on, grinning, and amazed me and Ogo by the speed their arms and fingers moved.

"Oh, let's dance!" said Ivar. "Money, Aileen. Give me money!"

"Me too," Ogo said. There was a crowd of fine-looking girls standing nearby, obviously waiting for partners. He and Ivar were already edging that way, but Ogo stopped to ask Finn politely if he was going to dance too.

Finn laughed and shook his head. "I don't think Green Greet would enjoy it."

"You could leave him perched on the cart," Ogo

was suggesting when Aunt Beck suddenly jerked her head up and glared at the dancers.

"What is this wickedness?" she said. "Stupid carrying on to music. Barbary"—she had taken to calling me Barbary, which was my mother's name—"Barbary, come away at once. Gran will half kill us if we stay here!" And she began trying to climb out of the cart.

"Stay where you are, Beck!" I snapped at her. "Gran isn't here."

"Then move the cart," she snapped back. "We can't stay here. Gran will find out."

Moe seemed to share my aunt's opinion. Her ears were flopping in protest at the music, and it looked as if she was working up to start braying. And when a donkey brays, you can hear little else.

I hurriedly got her moving again. "Did your grandmother really forbid *dancing*?" I said.

"Of course she does," Aunt Beck replied. "It's sinful and harmful. And," she added, thinking about it in her new strange childish way, "it's most undignified as well!"

Well, I knew my great-grandmother had had a name for being the most joyless woman in Skarr, but I had always thought this meant that she moaned and complained. But forbidding people to dance! That was ridiculous. "And did she forbid singing too?" I asked.

"Always," said my aunt. "Singing is unnatural. Will you hurry up, Barbary, and get us away from this wicked place!" She half stood up, angry and anxious.

It was quite clear Aunt Beck would run away if I didn't *take* her away. Between her and Moe, I seemed to have no choice but to leave all the fun.

As Moe got moving, Finn came trotting after us with one hand up to keep Green Greet steady on his shoulder. "What should we be doing, Young Wisdom?"

So I was Young Wisdom now, I thought. That put me horribly in charge. I tugged a fistful of coins out of the purse and shoved them into Finn's chubby hand. "Share that three ways," I said, "so that you and Ivar and Ogo can go to the Fair. I'm going down to the harbor to ask about the ferry. Meet me there in two hours." As

I said it, Moe fairly scampered away, before it occurred to me that none of us had a timepiece of any kind. While we rattled into the first streets of Charkpool, I saw myself waiting and waiting beside the sea and the ferry long gone for the day. Still, there was nothing I could do now, so I drove on with Aunt Beck sitting like a doll in the cart behind me.

Charkpool was a very orderly place. Not what I was used to in Bernica. It was all gray stone houses and quiet straight streets. I had no trouble finding our way to the harbor. There was a gate there, and people were streaming through it, all looking as if they were coming off the ferry and on their way to the Fair. I must say I was so glad to see the sea quietly lapping at the stone quayside that I did nothing for a minute but sit and stare at it, and at Gallis in the blue distance beyond, and breathe great breaths of the smell of it.

The man on the gate must have thought I was lost. "Was there something you were wanting, little lady?" he asked politely.

I think I jumped. "Oh," I said, still staring at the sea. It was blue-green here. "I was needing to take places on the ferry to Gallis for five people and this donkey and cart. Can you tell me where to do that?"

"Yes indeed," he said. I could see him looking to see what I was staring at. "Those ships are all out of commission these days, you know. There is no trade with Logra since the barrier went up."

This made me feel foolish. There was quite a line of tall ships almost in front of me, which I had been seeing without seeing, if you take my meaning, while I stared at the sea beyond. Now I looked at the ships, I could see that they were all but derelict, with green slime growing up their sides and most of their rigging gone. "I was wondering why they were so rotten-seeming," I said, to cover my foolish feeling. "Was there a lot of trade with Logra?"

"Day and night, little lady," he told me sadly. "Ten years ago every tide brought some dozens of ships into port, loaded with everything you could imagine. The barrier made for a lot of hardship. There's men I know, good sailors, who still have no work, though most of them have taken to fishing. It's a living of sorts. But the shops have gone, and the dockworkers. We're all too quiet now."

"That's very sad," I said.

"It is and all," he agreed. He was looking into the cart now at Aunt Beck. He was a nosy fellow. "Is your mother quite well in there? She's as quiet as Charkpool with the tide out."

"She's my aunt," I said. "And she's had a—had a stroke of—"

I was going to say "misfortune," but he misunderstood me. "Ah, a stroke, is it!" he said. "My cousin had one of those. Right as rain one moment, and the next he could hardly move a finger on his right side. Couldn't speak either. Is that why you have the beast in the cart, to guard her?"

I looked where he was looking, and Plug-Ugly looked back at me, plain to see in every spot. "Yes," I said.

"Perhaps you could direct me to the ferry?" I was beginning to think I'd never get there.

"Of course, of course," he said at once. "Just let me open the gate for you." He opened the gate, telling me all the while which bits of his cousin couldn't move, and then went with me down the dockside to show me the ferry. On the way he told at least six people that there was a poor lady in the cart who'd had a stroke and needed to get to Gallis. The result was that I sat in the cart for the next couple of hours, staring at the big bargelike ferry, while person after person came up and told me of parents, uncles, cousins, brothers, sisters, aunts, and friends who had suffered from strokes and what this had done to them. The really encouraging thing was that they nearly all said that the sufferer had gone on the ferry to Gallis and found a healer there to cure them. I realized it was true, as I had heard in Skarr, that the magics of Gallis were very potent. I began to hope someone there could lift the Lady Loma's spell. So I sat clutching the big bronze disk that was our ticket for the ferry, nodding and smiling eagerly at each person, and meanwhile getting very impatient indeed. The ferry was due to leave half an hour after midday, and I just could not see Ivar and Ogo tearing themselves away from the Fair in time.

But they did. It was Finn who achieved it somehow. They all arrived soon after noon, when passengers were already trickling aboard the ferry, all very pleased with themselves. Finn had been at his monkly cadging. He had an armload of food and a charm bracelet that he said would cure Aunt Beck. He insisted on fastening it around her wrist, in spite of her saying, "I won't wear that. It's unseemly."

Ivar was waving a pottery plaque with a blurred green bird on it. He had won a swordfight competition and was highly delighted with himself. "I beat ten other fellows!" he kept saying. "Beat them hollow!" But the real reason for his joy was that he had had his fortune told. "So I'll be coming with you to Gallis, after all," he said, but he wouldn't tell me why.

"I thought it was settled that you were coming anyway," I said.

"Not to me, it wasn't," he said. "Not until I heard what this seer had to say."

Ogo had had his fortune told too, it seemed. "But it was all nonsense," he told me. And he whispered, "Ivar won because the other swordsmen were so bad, actually, but don't tell him. Even *I* could have won if I'd gone in for it."

"What did you do instead?" I asked.

"Danced a bit. Went round the stalls," Ogo said. "They had a calf with two heads and a bird like Green Greet that sort of sang. Some of the things they were selling were really good. Like this. Look." He pulled out a rainbow scarf that seemed to be made of cobwebs and wrapped it tenderly around Aunt Beck's neck.

Aunt Beck blinked a bit and, to my surprise, she said, "Thank you kindly, young sir." She didn't seem to know it was Ogo.

"And this is for you," Ogo said, proud but

embarrassed. And he passed me a flat wooden box.

"Oh, you shouldn't have spent your money on me," I said as I opened the box. "Oh!" Inside was a necklace of copper plaited with silver with big green stones in it every so often. It was quite lovely. "It's beautiful!" I said.

"It wasn't expensive," Ogo said, rather pink. "I watched the woman make it. She was ever so clever. And I thought you needed something to make up for missing the Fair."

"It's the most splendid thing I've ever had!" I said. "*Thank* you, Ogo." And I put it round my neck. It was perfect, as if I'd had it always. I felt like a queen in it.

Then we had to board the ferry. They put a wide gangplank out because there were two more carts and a pony trap beside ours, and all three of these went up with no trouble at all. Moe refused. She braced all four hooves and went stiff. Ivar smacked her on the rump, and it made no difference at all. In the end Ogo and I had to walk backward on either side of her, hauling her bridle, with Finn and Ivar awkwardly leaning across the shafts to push on her rear. Like that, we inched onto the ferry. The sailors were fussing about the tide and the wind by the time we got her aboard. She really did not want to go. This surprised me. Up to then Moe had been such a good donkey.

They may call donkeys stupid, but in actual fact they are quite clever. Moe had stood and looked at the sea and the ferry and put two and two together. She must have known we were taking her away from the country of her birth. At all events, when they cast off the ropes and the sails filled and the ferry went rocking out into the wider water, the other two donkeys and the pony were given their nose bags and seemed quite content. Moe refused hers. She shook all over. Then she started to bray. Now the bray of a donkey, as I said before, is one of the loudest things in nature. It is a sort of roar, followed by a shriek of indrawn breath, followed by another roar. But the worst of it is that it sounds so *sad*. Poor Moe sounded heartbroken.

"Will you shut that donkey up!" the other passengers said.

"She really is heartbroken," I said. Ogo and I tried everything we knew to comfort her. We pulled her ears and petted her and murmured consoling things, but she brayed on and on.

Finally Finn said, with his hands over his ears, "She's afraid of the sea, so she is. Green Greet, can you settle her?"

"Can try," Green Greet said. And he flew up off Finn's shoulder and landed on Moe's head. She shook her head and flopped her ears, but he stayed on her. He started talking to her in a low, warbling murmur. It didn't have words. It was sort of animal talk. And after a bit Moe stopped yelling in order to listen. By the time we could see Gallis properly all lit by the sun, Green Greet had got Moe almost as quiet as the pony. He moved down her back and went on warbling to her, while the rest of us stared out at Gallis.

❧ X ❧

Gallis is very beautiful. The blue peaks and sunlit rifts full of trees assured us of this, but when the ferry swung into a glassy bay under the nearest blue peak, none of us could really attend to the scenery. Or perhaps Aunt Beck could, jolted this way and that as she sat in the cart we all tugged and pushed. Moe did not want to get off the boat. It was exasperating.

"Typical donkey," Ivar growled. "Shall I twist her tail?"

"No!" Ogo and I said together. "She's a Bernica donkey," I said. "She knows Gallis is a foreign country."

"Well, if you two want to be soft, slushy idiots, I'm not helping you anymore," Ivar said, and he went marching away down the gangplank. We could see him striding ahead up the rocky way that curved round the great mountain. Ogo and I exchanged looks. Both of us were hot and angry by then.

"Peace!" said Finn, which irritated me almost as much. "Let Green Greet guide Moe."

He shoved the bird off Moe's back quite unceremoniously. Green Greet, after an indignant squawk, flapped up ahead of Moe. He left a green feather, which Ogo picked up and put in his belt for luck. And Moe took off after Green Greet in a rush. Aunt Beck swayed about in the cart as it rattled down the gangplank, and we trotted after.

There was no real jetty, just a shelf of rock with a couple of bollards on it that the ferry tied up to. Everyone had gone streaming up the rocky path, so we followed, uphill and round the mountain. It reminded me of Skarr. Most of our bays are like this, except where the towns are. The difference was that Gallis was almost violently beautiful. The path led through a mighty gorge overhung with splendid trees, where a great white waterfall dashed down the cliffs to the left. On a ledge beside the waterfall we saw the distant figure of a man in blue clothes.

"What's he doing up there? It's not safe!" Aunt Beck said.

"He's playing the harp, Auntie," I said. "I think he's singing too."

You could just hear the music through the sound of the waterfall. And it was the strangest thing. As the song went on, the sun came out and made the trees green-gold. The falls shone silver-white with rainbows round the water, and the rocks glowed with colors.

"Have I got this right?" Ogo asked. "Is he singing the place more beautiful?"

"I think he is," Finn said, puffing rather. The path was steep. "I have heard many wonders of the bards of Gallis."

I had heard wonders too. People in Skarr always said that there was no magic like the magic of the bards of Gallis. They could sing anything to happen, they said, though I remembered my father laughing when I asked him about it and saying that he wished it were true. Some of it must have been, I thought, as we toiled round another corner and lost sight of the gorge and the bard.

"He *is* a bard," I said. "They always wear blue."

As I spoke, we came to a stone building and a gate across the path. Green Greet gave another squawk and landed on the gate, which seemed to alarm the man guarding it, who put up one thick arm to shield his face.

Ivar was standing angrily on our side of the gate. "He won't let me through!" he said to me. "He says I'm a foreigner. Make him see sense, Aileen."

"And he had no reason to insult me!" the guard said, backing away from Green Greet, but holding the gate shut as he went. He was a tall man and thick with it. He wore official-looking gray clothes and a sword. "I'm only doing my duty. I could see at once the young gentleman was not a native of Gallis, wearing plaids and all, as he is—"

"I *told* you. I'm a prince from Skarr," Ivar said. He was a little mollified by being called a young gentleman, but still angry.

"—and it is as much as my place here is worth to let him through—to let any of you through—before Owen the priest has examined you," the guard said, as if Ivar had not spoken. "I can see you're all foreigners. I have rung the bell, and Owen will no doubt be out presently. He's busy blessing the other travelers from the ferry."

"So we wait, do we?" Ivar snarled.

"In patience," the guard agreed. "Will one of you please remove the bird. I am not sure it is godly."

"Godly!" exclaimed Finn. "Nothing could be *more* godly than Green Greet! I begin to see that Moe was quite right not to wish to come to Gallis!"

"And which of you is Moe?" asked the guard.

"The donkey," Finn explained. "This donkey protested every yard of the voyage."

"Are *you* trying to insult me too?" the guard said, glowering.

"No, no!" Finn protested hastily. "I am a monk and a man of peace."

"Then move the bird," said the guard.

I found my spirits sinking steadily. I had forgotten the other thing my father always said of Gallis. I remember him praising the beauty of Gallis and its lovely climate often and often, until I asked him why, if Gallis was that wonderful, he had chosen to come away to Skarr. His reply was always "Because, Aileen, a person can do nothing in Gallis without the permission of a priest." I began to fear that our journey had come to a stop.

I watched Finn coax Green Greet onto his shoulder, and we waited for the priest.

Eventually the Holy Owen strode pompously up to the gate in a swirl of gray robes. I could see he was worse than the Priest of Kilcannon. He had rather a fat face decorated with a mustache even larger than the guard's. It must have got in the way when he ate. He folded his hands into the sleeves of his robe and leaned on the gate.

"Well, well," he said. "What have we here? Five foreigners and their livestock."

Livestock! I thought. At that moment I felt Plug-Ugly press invisibly against my legs. It made me feel much better.

"Green Greet," Finn said, as indignant as I had ever known him, "is *not* livestock, holy sir. He is the Great Bird of—"

"And you are?" Holy Owen said, cutting across him contemptuously.

"I am Finn," Finn said, "a monk of the Order of the Goddess from Bernica, and we are on a holy mission—"

"And you, madam?" Holy Owen said, cutting across poor Finn again. He looked up at Aunt Beck, sitting in the cart. "Are you in charge of this holy mission?"

Aunt Beck simply sat and said nothing.

Holy Owen waited for her to speak, and when she

did not even look at him, he narrowed his eyes at her. "Dumb, eh?" he said. "Then who *is* in charge?"

"I am," I said, before Ivar could open his mouth.

Holy Owen looked at me incredulously. I wished I was not so *small*. "Indeed?" he said. "And who may *you* be?"

I said, "My name is Aileen, and I am a Wise Woman of Skarr."

Holy Owen began to look downright derisive. "She is!" Finn and Ogo said together, and Finn went on. "The Great Lady herself declared Aileen to be fully initiate."

"Hmm," said Holy Owen. He went quickly on to Ivar. "And you?"

Ivar, not unnaturally, began proudly: "I am a prince of Skarr. My father—"

"Another foreigner," Holy Owen said dismissively. "You, great tall lad. Are you from Skarr, or Bernica?"

"Neither," Ogo said, almost as proudly as Ivar. "I'm from Logra."

"Logra!" exclaimed Holy Owen. "How did you get *here?*"

"I was left behind on Skarr when the barrier was raised," Ogo explained.

Holy Owen frowned at Ogo disbelievingly.

"It's true," I said. "He was quite small then."

Ivar said, "Yes, it's true. He's here as my servant."

"Fitting," Holy Owen said, and pulled at his huge mustache, considering us. "And the lady in the cart?"

"She is my Aunt Beck," I said, "and she is also a Wise Woman of Skarr." I had a moment when I seriously wondered whether to say that Aunt Beck was in a holy trance but thought better of it. Instead I said, "She suffered a stroke in Bernica. We were told that a holy healer of Gallis might be able to help her."

Holy Owen went "Hmm" again and continued to stare up at Aunt Beck and pull his mustache. "Miracles have been granted," he said. "But there is a problem. You are all five foreigners to Gallis."

Ivar, Ogo, and Finn all spoke at once. "But this is

ridiculous! People come from Bernica to be healed all the time. What are your healers for?"

And Green Greet echoed them. "Healers. Ridiculous."

I felt Plug-Ugly push against my legs. I said loudly, "Excuse me, holy sir, but this is not so. My father was born in Gallis. He is a bard."

Holy Owen let go of his mustache and looked sharply at me. "A small man, I suppose. What is his name?"

"Gareth," I said. I know I spoke as proudly as Ivar. "I remember him as quite tall."

"Gareth," Holy Owen said. "Him. He is well known here for going against all the advice of all the priests. It is also well known that he was snatched away with Prince Alasdair and taken to Logra."

"I know," I said. "I hope to find him someday. But you cannot deny that I am half a citizen of Gallis, and I lead this expedition. I think you must let us all through, holy sir, and bless us on our way."

There was a long silence. We all looked tensely at Holy Owen, who did nothing but stare at the gate and pull his mustache. Moe began to flick her ears and stir impatiently. At length Holy Owen went "Hmm, hmm"—twice for a change. "There is still a problem," he said. "If you were all from Bernica, I might solve it myself by sacrificing this donkey. But with people from both Skarr and Logra, I— Yes, I must seek advice from High Holy Priest Gronn. We are lucky. He is presently in this area adjudging the Singing Contest. I will send a messenger to him. Meanwhile, I must ask you all to stay inside the gatehouse until word comes back."

And this is what happened. We all protested. We argued. Ivar drew his sword. But more guards came out of the stone building before he could use the sword, and that was that. I grew angrier and angrier. I could see just why my father had left Gallis and come to Skarr. By the time we had been surrounded and urged into the courtyard inside the gatehouse, I was so angry that I felt a kind of power to me.

"Stop that!" I shouted to the guards who were unhitching Moe from the cart.

They stopped. They stared at me and then at Holy Owen. "And why should they stop?" Holy Owen asked me.

"Because I don't know what you're going to do with my donkey," I said.

"Nothing, only take it to the stables," Holy Owen said.

"How can I be sure of that?" I said. "When only five minutes ago you were talking of sacrificing her! I insist on going to the stables with her and making sure they look after her properly!"

Holy Owen sighed. "You Wise Women must be quite a pest to the Kings of Skarr. No wonder they turned you both out. Very well." He turned and beckoned to another, younger priest. "Go with her to the stable and make sure she behaves herself. You, guards, take the rest of them inside."

"I'm coming to the stables too," Ogo said.

I was very grateful. I felt myself beaming at Ogo as I said to Ivar, "Can you take care of Aunt Beck, then? Find her somewhere to sit."

Ivar scowled at me. But he nodded and took hold of my aunt's arm.

Aunt Beck said, "Let go of me, boy! I can walk on my own." And she went stalking ahead of Ivar to the dark doorway of the building.

"Queer sort of stroke," the young priest said as I led Moe off to the stables at the side. He was all dark hair and long nose with a drip on the end. I didn't like him. His name was Lew-Laws, it seemed. I was glad Ogo was there.

By the end I was *very* glad Ogo was there. The guard who was supposed to see to Moe obviously had no idea how to treat a donkey. I was forced to push him aside and look after Moe myself. Lew-Laws did nothing but lean against the side of the stall as if the whole matter was beneath him. Ogo loomed over the guard. This was the first time that I realized that Ogo had become very big indeed while we traveled, and very useful that was. Ogo loomed at the guard to fetch clean water. Then he loomed again to make sure he got Moe a decent amount of food, while I brushed her down and oiled the places where the harness rubbed her.

"Her hooves need trimming," Lew-Laws remarked unpleasantly. "Aren't you going to see to those too?"

Ogo, in the friendliest way, came and leaned against the wall next to Lew-Laws and loomed over him too. "I tried to do that in Bernica," Ogo said. "She doesn't like it. She kicks, but do find a file and try if you want."

Lew-Laws eyed Moe's hind hooves and moved away along the wall. "Not important," he said.

We left Moe pretty comfortable and let Lew-Laws take us into the house to a small room where Holy Owen sat at a table writing. Someone rushed in with a chair for Aunt Beck as we arrived.

"Good," Ivar said. "At last. I kept asking."

Aunt Beck sat down in the blank way that was now usual with her. I was disappointed. For a moment I had thought she was back to herself again. But no.

I went and put both hands on Owen's table. "How long will your message to Holy Gronn take?" I asked him.

"Hush," he said. "I am just now writing it. The messenger will be with him before midnight. I should have his reply by morning."

"You mean you're going to force us to spend the night here?" I exclaimed.

"Of course," he said. "Now tell me: this bird. Your monk calls him Green Greet. Why is that?"

"Because that's his name," I said.

Holy Owen shrugged and wrote. "I always heard," he muttered as he wrote, "that Green Greet was the great spirit of Bernica. Lord of the West. It's as bad as people calling their lizards Dragonlady, if you ask me."

He blotted the letter, folded it, and gave it to one of the guards.

"Make the best time you can," he said, "and be sure to explain that we need an answer by the morning."

"Thank you," I said.

Looking back on it, I see they did not treat us too badly. It was just that I disliked Holy Owen, and before long, I disliked Lew-Laws even more. Holy Owen went away after he had given the guard the message, and we did not see him again. But Lew-Laws stayed with us all the time. He had obviously been told to keep an eye on us, and he kept sighing about it as if it were a real burden.

"What do they think we're likely to *do*?" Ivar whispered angrily to me. "Make off with their valuables?"

"What valuables?" I said, looking round the bare stone room. We never knew the answer to that one, but as I said, we were not badly treated. Supper was delivered to the room, and it was a truly delicious fish stew. There were tastes in it that I had never met before.

While I was bullying Aunt Beck to eat it, Ogo said to Lew-Laws, "What are these lovely flavors? I remember something like this from Logra."

Lew-Laws sighed. "Herbs," he said. "I hate them.

They grow the things down south where they grow the vines and the olives and things. I wish they'd never been invented."

Lew-Laws was like that all the time. A wet week. Nothing pleased him. By bedtime I was truly depressed. I could not see our mission succeeding. I could not see any way Aunt Beck could be cured. "Take your stockings off, Beck!" I shouted at her, and I saw myself shouting at her like this for the rest of both our lives.

It was like that again in the morning. I shouted my aunt into her clothes, and we went back to the bare stone room to find Lew-Laws making faces as he drank some kind of hot herb tea that went with the bread for breakfast. When Ivar and Ogo had come yawning in, Lew-Laws sighed and said, "High Holy Gronn needs to see you. The gods alone know why. I am to take you to The Singing as soon as you have eaten. For my sins."

"Are you very sinful?" Ogo asked, mock innocently. Ivar tried not to laugh.

Before Lew-Laws could answer, Aunt Beck said,

"Where's my porridge? I can't start the day with bread."

"Ah," Lew-Laws said, "if I knew where to find porridge in Gallis, I would be a happy man, my good woman."

"No, really? A happy man?" Ivar said.

Lew-Laws pretended not to hear. "Bread," he said, "is what we eat here, woman. It's stale of course, but that is what there is."

"Eat it, Beck," I said. "You'll be hungry if you don't."

"Then I need butter," my aunt said. "And honey."

Finn came in at this point with Green Greet on his shoulder. "Green Greet will eat the bread for you," he said. "They've no seeds of any kind for him in the kitchen. No nuts either. And did you know," he asked Lew-Laws, "that some great beast got into the kitchen in the night and ate all the fish stew in the cauldron?"

Plug-Ugly, I thought. Oh, dear.

Lew-Laws sighed. "It is not my place," he said, "to criticize the gods if they choose to deny us fish for breakfast—"

"Where's my butter?" said Aunt Beck.

"Did the beast eat all the butter too?" Ogo asked.

"Butter is always scarce." Lew-Laws began dismally. "I haven't had butter since—" He was interrupted by a cross-looking servingman arriving with a bowl of oil— olive oil, he told me—to dip the bread in. This was just as well. Ivar choked trying not to laugh, and Ogo had to hammer him on the back. I would have been quite as bad, except that I was busy dipping bread for Aunt Beck and trying to persuade her that it was quite as good as porridge. She did eat some. What she left, Green Greet pecked up with enthusiasm.

Half an hour later we were on the road. Moe seemed none the worse for her night in the gatehouse and trotted along with a will. Ivar drove. Lew-Laws sat behind him, leaning over his shoulder to tell him the way. Aunt Beck sat upright behind Lew-Laws, and the rest of us walked. It was a lovely warm sunlit day, and we went by a route where waterfalls sparkled down beneath stately trees. I felt almost cheerful, despite the fact that we were going to meet someone who was obviously an important priest.

After a while we came out beside a long valley with a blue lake winding through it. There were islands in the lake, each one with its own little forest. As we looked, a shower of rain drifted across the end of the lake like the white ghost of a cloud. It was so beautiful that I started listening. And sure enough, the thread of song came distantly from somewhere.

"Do they *really* need a bard to make this place more beautiful?" Ogo said.

"Of course they do," Lew-Laws answered him. "There is mining at that end of the lake, and quarrying. Most unsightly."

"And we can't have that," Ivar said.

"Necessary evils," Lew-Laws said, not realizing Ivar was mocking him. "Gallis is an ugly place. All mountains. Almost nowhere is flat. Take this right turn of the road now."

That turn led us round the skirts of a mountain and

then out above another valley. This one was wide and flat and green with a long white building in the mid-distance, where people in bardic blue were flocking about.

"This place is flat," Ivar said. "Does that please you better?"

Lew-Laws sighed. "Not really. The ground is nothing but marsh in winter. The wind cuts through like a knife."

"But it's dry now," Ivar said, "and there's only a breeze."

"A man can catch his death, standing out there in the rain," Lew-Laws answered glumly. "They sing in all weathers. Draw the cart onto the grass here. We have to wait, no doubt for hours."

"Man of Ballykerry," Green Greet said suddenly.

Finn chuckled as the cart went bumping across the turf. "The man of Ballykerry," he said to Ogo and me, "was said never to be happy unless he was miserable, and even then he was not content."

Ogo laughed. I tried to, but I was suddenly

struggling with strong homesickness. There were high gorse bushes growing all around, and the smell of their flowers seemed to hit me to the heart. I longed so to be on Skarr and smell the gorse there that I could have cried. Lew-Laws directed Ivar to put the cart beside a big clump of several gorse bushes. For the next hour or so the smell seemed to fill my mind until I could think of almost nothing else.

Meanwhile, below in the valley a bell rang out from the white building. There were three silvery clangs, and then, as the sound went shimmering away into silence, people came swarming out from the white building. Some formed up into groups, large and small. About half were in bardic blue. Others wore wore a pale blue-green. Others again wore clothes of all colors, and they quietly spread themselves out along the edges of the green space as spectators. When everyone was in place, priests in gray came out of the building in a solemn procession. They stopped by the first group. One of the priests waved, and that group burst into song.

They sounded quite beautiful, fifty or so voices in harmony, but when the priests moved on to the next group and this lot sang the same song, I began to lose interest. By the fourth group I was trying not to yawn.

"Tell those people to stop that noise," Aunt Beck said. "They're giving me a headache."

Moe must have felt the same. As the fifth group began the song, she threw up her head and gave a mighty "hee-squeak-*haw!*"

The song stopped. Everyone down in the field turned to look at us.

"Hee-scream-haw!" Moe went, louder than ever.

"For the love of the gods, stop her!" Lew-Laws said. "Oh, I knew you were going to embarrass me. Such ungodly noises!"

Ogo leaped to the cart, seized Moe's nose bag, and crammed it on her face. That stopped her. The group began the song again, but it was not very good. There were wobbly sounds as though some of the singers were struggling not to laugh. The priests moved on to the next group, looking dour.

There were eight more groups. Moe ate and kept quiet for these, but Aunt Beck did not. She put her hands over her ears and said, "Will you go and get them to stop?" over and over, and Lew-Laws kept saying, "Woman, will you hush now!" until I wanted to hit them both.

Then it appeared that the next part of the program was to be singers on their own. A man in bardic blue stepped forward with a small harp on his arm. He sang long and sweetly, and at the end the spectators all applauded. It seemed they were allowed to do that now. After him came a girl in the pale green-blue who sang even longer but not so sweetly, and she was applauded too.

"What do they think they're pleased about?" Aunt Beck said loudly. "She sounds like a rusty door hinge."

"Oh, *hush*," Lew-Laws implored her. "This is torment to me, woman."

Moe began to show signs of restlessness again. We

managed to keep her quiet for the next four singers, but it was the applause that bothered her, really. When the seventh singer stepped forward, I looked round for Green Greet. Rather to my surprise he was perched on Ogo's shoulder and bending round to make little crooning noises at Ogo's face.

"Green Greet," I said, "*could* you be kind enough to keep Moe quiet?"

Green Greet bent himself round the other way to give me one of his wise, wrinkled looks. "Can do," he said. He sailed over to land on Moe's back, leaving a long green feather in Ogo's hair. Moe jumped at the feel of the bird on her back and tossed her head. "Silence," Green Greet said to her. "Eat your dinner, eat your dinner." And Moe did, to my relief, just as the seventh singer began her song.

It took only seconds for even Aunt Beck to realize that this lady was in a class by herself. The song soared, as clear as the notes of the silver bell, and sank, and mounted again as the words required, like the flight of the most glorious bird one could imagine.

"Much nicer," Aunt Beck said loudly. "I can even hear the words."

"*Shush!*" we all said, Green Greet included.

The song went on. I felt more than a little envious. I have never ever been able to hold a tune. Ivar laughs at me when I try. To make it worse, the singer was young and fair-haired and slender and—as far as I could see at that distance—decidedly beautiful. I sighed.

Finally the song ended. When it did, there was a moment of utter silence, as if the audience were too rapt to react. Then the applause was thunderous. People shouted and stamped as well as clapping. Aunt Beck actually clapped too.

And Moe somehow got her head out of the nose bag and joined in with a bray. But by then it didn't matter. The chief priest, who I assumed must be High Holy Gronn, advanced on the girl, still clapping, and then stopped clapping in order to pin a shining brooch of some kind on the front of her green-blue tunic.

When the applause began to die away, another priest announced in a huge, rolling voice, "The winner of The Singing is Riannan at the Pandy." And the applause began again and went on until my hands were quite sore.

High Holy Gronn suddenly appeared beside the cart. I suppose he must have hurried across while the applause was going on, but I was not sure. There was so much magic in Gallis. "Lew-Laws," he said, "did you *have* to bring a noisy donkey as well as a noisy woman?" and he laughed. Close to, Gronn turned out to be a small, tubby man with a round, merry face. This is the muddling way things turn out sometimes. I had been full of suspicion about the priests of Gallis and prepared to fight them every inch of our way, but I looked at High Holy Gronn and thought, Why, he's *nice*! It was quite confusing.

Lew-Laws of course went into an ecstasy of dismal respect. He wrung his hands and he writhed. "Oh, High Holy one," he protested, "I do apologize! They are the most ungodly crew. The woman is dotty, and her donkey is insane. I am not sure which of them is worse!"

"Then I relieve you of them all," High Holy Gronn said with a broad smile. "Your trials are over, and you can go straight back to the gatehouse."

Lew-Laws was utterly surprised. "What, now?" he said. "Without lunch?"

"You may pass by the caterers," Gronn said, "and ask them for a meat roll to eat on your way. Tell them I sent you. Go now." He watched Lew-Laws go sulkily off and shook his head. "That man," he said to us, "always reminds me of the man of Ballykerry in Bernica. Never happy. No matter. We always put the misfits to man the gatehouses. And now—" He looked us over one by one, not excluding Moe and Green Greet on her back. The only one of us he didn't see was Plug-Ugly, who chose that moment to press himself invisibly against my legs. I was glad of the feel, because Gronn's look was so very shrewd. His wide, wrinkling blue eyes seemed to sum us all up exactly. I supposed he could not have become High Holy without being exceedingly clever, but it was unnerving all the same.

His eyes finally went back to Finn. "You, sir," he said. "Come aside with me and tell me, as one holy man to another, precisely how and why you are all here in Gallis." He held out an arm and cheerfully ushered Finn some way off beyond the gorse bushes.

Finn is such a humble person. I could see he was surprised and dismayed to be singled out at first. But as soon as Gronn had led him out of earshot and smiled at him, I could see Finn begin to loosen up. Before long he was talking and gesturing as if he and Gronn had been friends for years. More Gallis magic, I thought, and I hoped Finn was telling it right.

"He should have chosen me," Ivar said. "I'm the Prince here."

"He was probably going by age," I said, to soothe him. But I suspected that Gronn had chosen Finn because he saw Finn was simple and honest.

They talked for some time. Long before they finished, Ivar and Ogo had been scanning the field to see where the caterers were and wondering if they would be allowed to have a meat roll like Lew-Laws. They made me feel peckish too.

"I could eat a pickled herring," Aunt Beck was announcing just as Gronn and Finn came back.

"Now there you have me, lady," Gronn said to her. "We have fresh crab and jellied eels, but the herring deserted Gallis waters after the barrier went up. Did you not know?"

Aunt Beck just stared at him. I could see Gronn looking at her carefully to see exactly what her state was before he turned to me. "That," he said, "is not a simple stroke, is it, Aileen? What made you tell Holy Owen it was?"

I felt my face turning red. "It—it was easier to explain," I said. "Not many people are going to believe that she was nearly turned into a donkey, are they?"

"By the Red Woman of Bernica?" Gronn said. I

nodded. Finn had told it right, it seemed. "You see," Gronn explained, "I need to know that before I decide who to send her to. An ordinary healer would be no good to her. But I'm working on it. Meanwhile the rest of you are Ivar, son of King Kenig from Skarr; Ogo, from Logra and Skarr; and Green Greet of Bernica. Have I got that right?"

And Plug-Ugly, I thought, feeling him against my legs.

Then Ogo *would* have to say, "And there's Plug-Ugly from what's left of Lone, sir." When Gronn stared at him, he turned redder than I was and stammered, "Bu—but—he's mostly invisible—honestly." I glowered at him.

Plug-Ugly made a small growl that could have been "Oh, well" and slowly, grudgingly turned visible beside my legs. Gronn stared at him and then looked over at Green Greet, who was now back on Finn's shoulder. He seemed impressed.

"And you are all on your way to raise the barrier

round Logra?" Gronn went on. "In that I wish you well, although I have no idea how you would do it." He turned to Finn, as the one most likely to understand. "There must be people dying on Logra because we cannot help them." Finn nodded sadly. Then Gronn turned to me. "And you, Aileen, besides being a Wise Woman of Skarr, are the daughter of my old friend Gareth, I gather?"

"Yes," I said. "Was he really your friend?"

"Oh, yes," said Gronn. "You would not believe the times we spent arguing about our system here in Gallis. But he was abducted along with Prince Alasdair, wasn't he? Is he still alive?"

"I don't know. I hope so," I said. "I want to find him."

"Well, it's possible. Impossible but possible," Gronn said. "And that puts all sorts of things into my head. Did you know you have cousins here?"

"I do? Here in Gallis?" I said. I was very surprised. My father had never talked much about his family, though I remembered he did once tell me a story about how he and his brother were chased by a bull on a neighbor's farm.

"Not only here in Gallis," Gronn said, beaming at the look on my face, "here in this very spot. Two of your cousins came for The Singing. Though I think Rees came to support Riannan. Not much of a singer, Rees. Wait a moment, and I'll have them fetched over."

~ XI ~

A boy in a gray coat was sent rushing off, with instructions from Gronn to fetch "a decent lunch," as well as these cousins of mine. The lunch arrived first. We all, including Gronn, sat on the grass to eat rolls stuffed with crab and big bunches of grapes. Ivar, Ogo, and I had never eaten grapes, though we all had had raisins. Gronn was explaining, in a very satisfied way, that grapes grew in profusion in the south of Gallis. I think he then went on to tell us they were dried into raisins to send to Skarr; but my cousins arrived then, and I am not sure.

Rees was good-looking and fair-haired, taller and older

than Ivar, and he seemed the most easily friendly person I have ever met. His sister, my cousin Riannan, was the very same girl who had won The Singing. I was awed. Close to, she was staggeringly lovely. I wondered how someone could have such huge blue eyes and delicate features—not to speak of a marvelous shape—and yet be so modest, even a little shy. Riannan smiled, looking down at the grass, then looked up, first at me, then at Ivar. After that she looked nowhere else. Ivar stared back. His face, with the thin beginnings of a beard, turned slowly crimson and then pale. And Riannan still stared. It didn't seem to matter to her that Ivar's hair had grown all shaggy or that his once-good clothes were now stained and old. It was plain that she thought he was perfect. And Ivar thought the same of her, all trim and lissome as she was, in her blue-green tunic with the starry brooch flashing on the front of it.

"Listen now," Gronn was saying when I brought my mind back, "we have this lady Beck who has been unfortunate with the Red Woman of Bernica and needs some healing help."

Rees gave Aunt Beck the same sort of professional, summing-up look that Aunt Beck normally gave other people. "A spell, is it?" he said.

"Indeed, yes," Gronn said. "A spell she has half resisted. Do you think Wenda could handle it?"

"My mother can handle most things," Rees said, grinning.

"Well, then," said Gronn, "this is what I'm suggesting: that you take them all back with you to the Pandy, introduce Aileen to her aunt and her Uncle Bran and so forth, and see what your mother can do for Beck." He said to me, "Wenda is my second cousin, and there is no one more capable of lifting spells than she is in all Gallis. If you set off now, you can avoid the crowds at the way stations. Will that suit you?"

"Oh yes, perfectly," I said, flustered. "Thank you." I saw that my aunt was sitting there in the cart not attending to anything, with a crab roll still in her hand. "Eat your lunch, Beck," I snapped halfheartedly. I was *so* sick of shouting at her.

"Well now," Gronn said, brushing crumbs off his rounded front, "I shall go back to my duties and leave you with my blessing." He smiled and made gestures in the air, which I supposed was his blessing, and then wandered gently away. He seemed to be down on the greensward and in the distance near the white building before he had taken three steps. The magic of Gallis again, I thought.

"No need to hurry," Rees said amiably. "Anyone care for some more lunch?" He held up the cloth bag he was carrying.

"Yes, please," Ogo said. He was always hungry.

Plug-Ugly was always hungry too. He advanced on Rees, tail swinging, and stood on his hind legs against Rees's knees with one large paw stretched toward the cloth bag. Rees laughed.

As Plug-Ugly's paw touched the bag, there was the tiniest hissing. I saw two bright red eyes staring from the cuff of Rees's sleeve.

"Oh, have you got a pet rat?" I said. My cousin Donal had a rat when he was younger, which he used to let climb about inside his clothing. And the truth was, I was prepared to be interested in *anything* to keep my mind off Ivar and Riannan.

Rees laughed again. "No, not a rat," he said. He shook his arm a little, and a tiny red lizard ran out, long and thin, and raced up his sleeve to his shoulder, where it coiled round and glared down at Plug-Ugly.

"Oh!" I said.

"Her name is Blodred," Rees said. "She's a dragon-lizard."

"They're very common here in Gallis," Riannan said. "A lot of people make pets of them. Rees has had Blodred since he was five years old. Don't you have them in Skarr?"

"No," we all said. Finn added, "Nor in Bernica, but I've heard of them. I think it may be too cold for them north of Gallis."

Ogo leaned above me to look closely at the lizard. It really could have been a tiny dragon. It had a sort of frill that looked like wings on its faintly pulsing red sides. "Does she fly?" Ogo asked.

"No, not really," said Rees. "Those are not proper wings—just skin she can spread a bit and glide on. And," he added proudly, "they come in all colors, but red is the very rarest."

We all sat down again and had more lunch. Ivar and Riannan sat close together and talked to each other in little broken sentences. As far as I could tell, she was asking about Ivar's life on Skarr and he was trying to compliment her on her singing. In between, they stared at each other as if they were seeing the most marvelous thing in the world. And they both blushed a lot.

All in all, I was quite glad to concentrate on making Aunt Beck eat. Then I was pleased that Plug-Ugly was behaving rather badly and trying to take crab away from people. I don't think that there had been any crab in his life before this, and he discovered he had a passion for it. I had to shout at him—not that it made much difference. After that, I kept my attention on Blodred, who was eating tiny shreds of crab she held in her delicate red fingers. I even watched Green Greet pecking away at an apple turnover.

It was a relief to me when Rees said we had better get moving.

"Aileen, you drive," Ivar said.

So I climbed into the cart and took the reins, while Rees went ahead with Ogo and Finn to show the way. We went through uplands of perfect beauty, where streams poured musically over rockfalls covered with wild flowers while blue peaks towered behind, and all I could think of was Ivar and Riannan walking behind, talking in murmurs and laughing. There were gaps in the peaks we went through, where I could see the sea, blue as Riannan's eyes, or lakes in valleys or, on one occasion, a huge golden view of Gallis stretching away southward, full of fields and distant orchards. Moe did not like this. She shook her ears and made it plain she was not used to mountains. But all I could think of was Ivar and Riannan walking behind.

We stayed that night at a way station. It was a sort of

barn with wooden bunks and a hearth in it. There was another hearth outside where you could cook any food you had brought with you and a well for water. We sat outside and ate crab again. Gallis is so beautifully warm that we could have *slept* outside if we wanted to.

There are no inns in Gallis, Rees told us. There are wineshops and drinking places down on the plains, all carefully regulated by the priests. You can only drink within certain hours, he said. "But it's much more relaxed than it used to be, now Gronn is High Holy," he told us. "Gronn's long talks with Gareth made quite a difference to his outlook." Then he told us other customs of Gallis, which I now forget. I was trying not to notice Ivar attending only to Riannan. Aunt Beck simply sat. Finn yawned. Ogo was the only one who really listened to Rees.

We went on next morning through more lovely mountain scenery. The way was steadily uphill, and Moe was not happy. Ogo and I had to take hold of her bridle on either side and positively haul her along. Rees and Finn drew farther and farther ahead. Ivar and

Riannan, though loitering, were well in front too.

"Oh, come *on*!" I told Moe crossly.

"I'm doing the best I can," Aunt Beck said from the cart.

"I didn't mean *you*!" I snapped. Then I found I was crying. Big tears ran down my face, and I gulped as if I were choking.

Ogo said, "Don't be unhappy, Aileen."

"I can't *help* it!" I snarled. "Here's my aunt gone back to childhood and left me to manage everything and we keep traveling and journeying and I haven't the *least* idea how we'll get to Logra and I don't think I'll find my father! *Ever!*"

"Oh, we'll get there," Ogo said. "Somehow. After all, we have the Beast of Skarr on our side *and* the Great Bird of Bernica. And now we even have a Dragon of Gallis too, though I admit she's a bit tiny."

I stared at Plug-Ugly plodding ahead of me up the track, long legs, small head, ugly markings, and all. Not to speak of smelling of crab. I shoved my sleeve across my wet eyes and stared again. "You don't mean—"

"Yes, I do," Ogo said. "You can't deny he's fairly magical. And Green Greet talks sense, not like other parrots. Remember old Alison and Kendal's parrot? It only ever says, 'Hello, me darlin'' or 'Give us a nut' and things. Green Greet knows what he's saying."

"I suppose you're right," I said, beginning to feel rather awed. "We might have at least two of the Guardians with us, then."

"So we'll get to Logra and find your father," Ogo said, "if he's still to be found. And I had a feeling you were quite enjoying being in charge—"

"Not when I couldn't dance at the Fair," I said.

"But most of the time," Ogo said. "Come on. Admit it. And you shouldn't make yourself miserable over Ivar, you know. He's not worth it."

I hadn't realized my feelings had been that obvious. "I'll have you know, Ogo of Logra," I said, "that I chose Ivar long ago to be my husband!"

"I know," Ogo said. "But you were small then, and

he seemed quite grown up. I've been hoping for years you'd see your mistake."

"*Mistake!*" I almost shrieked.

"Gran always says you make mistakes," Aunt Beck said from the cart.

"Be quiet, Beck," Ogo said. "Yes, a mistake. You have brains, Aileen. Ivar's really quite stupid. You'd be bored stiff if you had to be with him all the time. I know I am. He seems to think that being a prince makes him perfect."

I thought about this. I suppose I had never credited Ivar with brains. Donal was the one with brains, and I had always known this was the reason Mevenne preferred Donal to Ivar. But she gave Ivar anything he wanted, all the time. All the children at the castle knew there was no point having a disagreement with Ivar. He would go to his mother, and she would punish the person who disagreed with him. Thinking about it, I saw that this was Mevenne's way of making it up to Ivar for the fact that she was not very fond of him.

My earliest memories of Ivar were of being faintly sorry for him. Mevenne spoiled him rotten, but she never hugged him as she hugged his brother. Aunt Beck, who was not a hugging kind of person, hugged me whenever I needed it, and when I was small, she even used to take me on her (very bony) knees. Mevenne never did that to Ivar. But I believe Ivar thought he was her favorite. How silly!

"But Riannan is so beautiful!" I wailed.

"So are you," Ogo retorted.

I stared at him. "She has hair like ripe oats," I protested.

"Your hair," said Ogo, "is just the color of the toffee the castle kitchen makes on feast days. You should let it go loose oftener because it's all curly."

"It would get in my way," I said. "And she has big blue eyes."

"Your eyes are quite as big," Ogo said, "and they are green most of the time. I've never seen anyone else with eyes your color."

"But I'm so *short*," I said. "Riannan's nearly as tall as you."

"Quite a beanpole," Ogo said impatiently. "If you're determined to think of yourself as an ugly midget, go ahead. But don't expect me to sympathize."

I found I was laughing. "All right, all right," I said. "But there is one thing. I can't sing. And you heard Riannan."

"Yes, she can sing," Ogo said, "but she's not a Wise Woman, is she? And I don't suppose her voice has much to do with the way Ivar's feeling."

I laughed again, a little. We walked on. We must have gone nearly half a mile before it occurred to me to say, "Thank you, Ogo."

He grinned down at me. "You're welcome, Aileen."

He had made me feel so much better that I even began to look at the scenery. It was all rugged rock. There didn't seem to be a bard around to sing it beautiful, so it was as plain as Plug-Ugly and as gaunt and gray. I found it very comforting. It reminded me of Skarr.

Shortly, however, we came into an upland that was nearly level, where the grass was a normal kind of green. There were sheep grazing it everywhere. They wandered onto the road and stared at us and bleated. Round a bend there was fencing with cows behind it, and round the next bend there was a large rock. For some reason there was a rope wrapped round this rock with what looked like a small ship's anchor spliced to the end of it.

"Are they afraid the rock will fly away?" Ogo wondered.

"You never know, with all the magic in Gallis," I said.

As I said it, we came round the rock and saw that the rope led to a small shed uphill from us.

"No, it's the hut that might fly away," Ogo said.

Rees and Finn were waiting just beyond the hut. Ivar and Riannan joined them just as we saw them. They all turned and watched us coming.

"Welcome to the Pandy," Rees said when we drew level. He gestured uphill to the left.

There was a big old farmhouse there, surrounded by more sheep and nestled most comfortably among rocks and stone buildings. Someone in one of the doorways saw us coming and shouted and went dashing to the back of the house. By the time we arrived, the farmhouse door was open and Rees's mother and father were coming out to greet us, with, behind them, quite a crowd of farm workers and servingwomen.

"She won The Singing!" someone shouted. "I knew she would!"

Riannan's mother rushed to embrace her. Then we were all introduced, and a massive cowman reached into the cart and picked Aunt Beck out of it. She was carried into the Pandy, sitting demurely across his great arms, just as she had been carried to the boat in Skarr. Indoors we were all made very welcome. I think I have never felt so much at home as I did in that house.

The main room downstairs was a vast kitchen, very light because it was whitewashed. The wide windows looked out to the southwest. There was a fire in the big hearth, despite the warmth of the day, and the cowman installed Aunt Beck in a cushioned chair beside it before going crashing out through one of the several outside doors. There were big black beams in the ceiling with things hanging from them. Green Greet flew up there at once, where he sat gravely inspecting a string of onions. Plug-Ugly made straight for the fireside. Four sheep dogs and a whole crowd of cats instantly made room for him, most respectfully. He threw himself down in the best place, and in my memory, the rest of the day was filled with his rumbling purr.

I saw all these things in snatches because I was being passed between my uncle and aunt, who kept saying, "Really Gareth's daughter! You have quite a look of him!" and, "You have your father's eyes, did you know?" and so forth. It made me feel quite tearful. Wenda, my aunt, was almost as lovely as Riannan, except she was older, of course, and her hair was darker. My uncle's name was Bran. I kept looking to see if he resembled my father, but it was hard to tell because he was very tall and had a full beard besides. I think he had the same slight air of majesty that I remembered in my father, as if he were above most people without meaning to be in the least. Rees's younger brother, Brent, had the same air.

It was very strange to find so many unknown relations. And shortly there were more. People came flocking in from the houses down the other side of the hill, all on purpose to meet us. Each one would say to me things like "I'm your father's second cousin twice removed, see," or "I'm your grandmother's niece, you know." There were so many of these that I am quite unable to recall them all. The only ones I remember were the Dominie and the priest, who stayed to supper, and they were relatives too. The Dominie was Wenda's sister and very learned, even more erudite than the priest, who was Bran's cousin. Really, it reminded me of Skarr, the way everyone was related, and I had to struggle with another attack of homesickness.

All these visitors caused a great bustle of hospitality. Wine was brought out and tea was made, and Wenda and the two maidservants became very busy handing round olives and salty biscuits to go with the drinks. Ivar's face when he first tasted an olive was a picture. His cheeks sucked in, his mouth and eyes screwed up, and he said desperately, "Where can I spit this out? *Please!*"

Riannan collapsed with laughter but managed to say, "In the fire, of course, silly!"

Ogo said, "Oh, I remember these!" and took handfuls. He really loved them. And so, it seemed, did Aunt Beck. Ogo sat on a stool beside her chair and carefully took the hard little pipstones out of olive after olive for her. The fire hissed with a bombardment of olive stones. I think Ogo ate two for every one he gave Aunt Beck.

Finn sat quietly in a corner, eating everything that was offered. Well, I always thought Finn could eat *anything*. Me, I preferred the salty biscuits, although I imagined I might just acquire the taste for olives in time. Green Greet came down from the beams to share the biscuits with me.

In the intervals of all this, Finn, Ogo, and I were at

the windows, fascinated. Bran's farmland stretched away downhill into the sunlight in gentle shelves. The gray-green trees nearest were where the olives grew. But there were vineyards and orchards of more normal fruit beyond, and field after field of crops of all kinds; I recognized barley and hay, but many were plants I had never seen before. The most fascinating things, though, were teams of little fat horses pulling carts of produce to the barns. They were not exactly carts. They had no wheels. Each one seemed to float ponderously behind the team pulling it.

"How can that be?" Finn wondered.

I wondered too. But mostly I was thinking that Bran in his way had a kingdom out there, full of distant relatives, rather like my distant cousin King Kenig.

When all the visitors had gone except the priest and the Dominie, there was supper served around the huge table. While I was busy bullying Aunt Beck to eat, Ogo got very bold and chatty and kept asking questions. One of the first things he asked was what were the astonishing carts without wheels.

"Oh, those," Rees said, "are a magical invention of my father's. Neat, aren't they?"

I looked at my uncle, thinking, So he's a magician too!

Bran grinned. "Took me a while to think them up," he said. "They're easier on the horses. But I still haven't found a way to stop them swiveling about."

"They need careful driving," Riannan said. "I can't do it."

"No, my girl," Bran said. "I'm still shuddering at the way you crashed my first one into the big barn."

Riannan went very pink and said nothing more. Ivar, who would have laughed loudly at anyone else, looked at her sympathetically. "I can see it's an art," he said. I found I still seethed a little at that.

Ogo went on asking things, but the question I chiefly remember was when we were eating piles of pancakes covered with jam and honey for dessert. Ogo said, "Do you ever get snow here?"

"Not often," the Dominie said, and, typically of

a teacher, went on. "Gallis lies in a warm air current from the southern ocean, you see."

"But when it does snow," Ogo said, "what do the bards do?"

"Oh, they get really busy," Rees said, laughing. "They swarm around singing it all thick and white and picturesque, with beautiful icicles on every waterfall."

"Not on my farm, they don't," Bran said, and he and the priest exchanged slightly grim looks. I could see that he and the priest disagreed about the activities of the bards.

All through the meal Wenda had been looking at Aunt Beck in a deep, thoughtful way. "This is quite a strange spell she's under," she said to me. "But I'll see what I can do." And when supper was done, she took Aunt Beck away somewhere else in the house. The Dominie and the priest left, as if this were a signal, and the rest of us helped the maidservants clear away. While these girls sat down for their supper, Bran sent Brent to bed and led all the rest of us into a small parlor. Someone had lit a fire there as if we had been expected. Plug-Ugly padded after us and laid himself down in the warmth again.

"Right, Rees," Bran said. "Are you set on this?"

"More than ever," Rees replied. He had—somehow—come alight. I could see he had been holding himself in ever since we first saw him, and from probably before that. If Aunt Beck had been there and in her right mind, she would have said something like "He's been hiding his light under a bushel, hasn't he?" Now he was himself. His eyes shone, and he sat as if he were ready to leap out of his chair. "What I'm going to talk about is something very secret," he said. "The priests would call it ungodly."

Finn shifted about as he sat. "Are we in a conspiracy, then?" he asked. Green Greet leaned down from Finn's shoulder to stare into his face.

"Yes, I think so," Rees said. Blodred suddenly popped out from under his collar and stared at Finn too.

Finn swallowed. "I see that this is important," he said. "Would my goddess object?"

Bran said, with a small chuckle, "Be easy, man. One thing I have learned over the years is that what the priests say and what the gods think are quite often different things. We have a prophecy to guide us here."

"Ah," said Finn.

Rees leaned forward eagerly. "This is something I've been wanting to do for years. I want to rescue my uncle, who was stolen away with the prince of Skarr. I've been working on the *practical* way to do it all this year." He looked at me. "You want to see your father again, don't you?"

I felt as if a huge hand was squeezing my chest. I didn't know if it was excitement or terror. I managed to gasp out, "How—how—?"

"Now you are here, you can help," Rees said. "I was going to take four people from the Pandy, besides Riannan to sing us on, but you four are perfect. Will you agree to come?"

"Yes, but how are you planning to get through the barrier?" Ogo said. "Nobody else can."

Rees laughed. "We fly in," he said. "*Over* the barrier."

"But," I said, "but isn't the barrier like a dome over the whole of Logra?"

"It can't be," Rees declared. "If it was, Logra would have run out of air long ago, and the fishermen have seen people alive there. But if it *is* a dome, we just fly back here and think again. See, the wind sets from the west at dawn, which is when we'll go, and it sets from the east at sunset, so it will bring us back to Gallis."

"What kind of wings do you plan to use to fly to Logra?" Finn asked. "It's a fair way to go. We'd have to flap for miles."

"Over the sea too," Ogo said. "Some of us could drown."

Rees laughed again. He was almost hugging himself with delight. "No wings," he said. "I have made a balloon."

We all said, "*What?*" Even Ivar, who was in a corner with Riannan and not listening to a word up to then, came to himself and demanded to know what Rees was talking about.

"It rises by hot air," Rees explained, "and is made of silk. In Gallis we float small silk balloons at Midsummer by lighting a candle underneath. That gave me the idea. But I put one of Dad's floating carts under mine to help it fly. It will work."

"Have you tested it?" Ogo asked.

"Only in miniature, unfortunately," Bran told him. "You can just imagine what the bards and the priests would say if Rees went flying across Gallis without permission. We'd be turned out of the farm. But the small model worked like a dream. Flew like a kite. We told Gronn it was a kite."

"So," Rees said, "my very first flight will be tomorrow at dawn. Are you all willing to come along? I need two pairs of people, see, to man the bellows to keep the hot air going."

Bran sighed a little. "And he needs his dad to stay at home and pretend Rees and Riannan are walking to

the coast with you all. You are all going, aren't you?"
I could tell he was itching to fly too and knew that he
couldn't. He was as enthusiastic as Rees about the plan.

So were we all. Rees had carried us away with him
somehow. When I look back, I see it was a crazy idea.
We didn't even know if this balloon thing would work,
let alone if we could get all the way to Logra in it. But I
was on fire with the thought of seeing my father again,
and I could see Ogo ached to fly home to Logra. But
why should Finn agree? Or Ivar? And they both did.
Riannan I could understand. She admired her brother
so, and I think she wanted to prove that she could sing
magically enough to soar through the skies.

"What are our plans when we get to Logra?" Ivar
asked, just as if he were a practical person.

"Land in a field somewhere near the main city.
What's it called?" Rees said.

"Haranded," Ogo put in.

"Yes, Haranded," Rees said. "And go in on foot to
find Gareth and—what's that prince called?"

"Alasdair," I said.

"Alasdair, yes," Rees said. "I can't imagine they'll be guarded very closely after all this time. Then we take them back to the balloon at dusk and fly away. I've laid in enough fuel for the return journey, see."

And that was all our plans. We had got this far when Wenda came in, bringing my aunt with her.

"So you have truly decided to risk it?" she said, looking sadly around at our faces. "Ah, well. Beck can stay here with me. I've done what I can for her for the moment, but it's going to be a long job, I think. And of course we'll look after your donkey while you're gone. But if you change your minds in the morning, we shan't think the worse of you."

ᴄXIIᴄ

I thought I would be too excited to sleep that night, but in fact, I slept very well. Aunt Beck, though she looked no different, actually put herself to bed in the little room next to mine without my having to shout at her once. This was such a relief that I suddenly found myself quite exhausted. I fell among the soft covers of my bed and knew nothing until Riannan woke me before sunrise.

"Dress warm," she whispered. "It may be cold over the sea."

I put on my thickest good dress and took my coat with me down to the kitchen. Everyone was there, including Bran, to see us off. We ate bread and cheese while Wenda packed us a mighty bag of provisions. Blodred came out of Rees's sleeve to nibble some bread, and Green Greet stepped about on the table, pecking up anything anyone dropped. I could see he was making sure he was well fed for the journey. But there was no sign of Plug-Ugly. At first I thought, Oh, he's invisible again. I felt about, but I couldn't discover him anywhere, either under the table or by the dead fire.

There was a moment then when my confidence wavered. I thought, If Plug-Ugly won't trust himself to this balloon thing. . . . But I was too excited. We were going to fulfil our mission. And I ached to see my father again.

It was still blue-dark when we went out, down the track to the shed we had noticed on the way to the Pandy. Riannan raced down to the boulder and began unwinding the rope from it. Rees and Bran together took hold of the sides of the shed and lifted them away.

Inside, I could dimly see a great heap of many-colored silk, which Rees carefully dragged across the hillside until it was spread into a vast billowing round. It was attached by more ropes to a boat-shaped thing made of woven willow wands.

Someone was sitting in the boat. We peered. It was Aunt Beck.

Yes, there she was, very upright, calmly eating bread and cheese. Beside her was Plug-Ugly, chewing at a lump of meat.

"Beck!" we all exclaimed.

"High time you all came," she said. "Let's get going."

"But Beck," I said, "I don't think you should come with us."

"And there we were tiptoeing and whispering not to disturb you!" Ivar said disgustedly. "What are you *doing* here?"

Aunt Beck looked at him severely. "I have to get away from that donkey," she said.

Mad! I thought. But Wenda, who was helping

Riannan fix the anchor to a hole in the hillside, stood up and called out, "Oh, *now* I understand! That spell somehow tied her to that donkey of yours! She'd better go with you. It's the best way to break the connection."

So that was why Moe had been acting up, I thought, while Bran said anxiously, "Will this make the boat too heavy, do you think?"

"Not really," Rees said. "She's very skinny. She and Aileen together must weigh less than Pugh, who I was going to take. Pugh's husky. Light the fire, Dad. I want to catch the dawn wind."

Actually, I thought we'd never get off. The fire was in a sort of metal box in the middle of the boat. After Bran had lit the packed charcoal in it with—to my envy and admiration—a word and a flick of his fingers, Rees set Ogo and Ivar to working the foot pumps fastened to bellows under the box. The fire roared and went from blue to red to white. Riannan, Rees, Finn, and I had to hold the heavy silk up so that the heated air could get inside the balloon. It was oiled silk in many layers.

I was amazed at the work it must have taken. Silk was not easy to come by in Gallis. Rees told me that most of it came from Logra long ago. They had to collect it in a thousand small pieces and sew those pieces together. The balloon, when it finally began to bulge and lift a little, was a mad patchwork of raw parchment color, bardic blue, floral scarves, petticoat pink, and red wedding dresses, with even some embroidered panties in there somewhere.

"Oh, yes," Riannan told me, with sweat from the fire rolling down her fine fair hair, "it took us a whole year, sewing madly. Mother sewed, I sewed, Rees sewed. Rees was mad to get it finished before the priest noticed, see."

The envelope, as the crazy patchwork was called, took so long to fill that Wenda had plenty of time to go round and hug us all, before she had to stand by the anchor to unhook it from the hillside. Bran irritated Rees by hovering over the little lever that sent the wheelless cart up into the air underneath the boat.

"Is it time to switch it?" he kept saying. "Just say the word, son."

"Not *yet!*" Rees kept snapping. "Don't waste the spell."

Aunt Beck irritated everyone by saying, over and over, "Hurry up. Let's get going."

Even Finn, all pink and sweaty, bared his teeth at her and said, "Will you hold your noise, Wisdom, or I shall find myself getting Green Greet to peck you?"

But at last, at long last, the patchwork billows swelled themselves into a great ball shape and came upright off the hillside to float above the boat.

"Keep pumping!" Rees yelled at Ivar and Ogo, who both looked as though they might expire. Then he shouted to his parents, "Lever, Dad, *now!* Anchor, Mum. Oh, for Gallis's sake, *move,* both of you!"

I think Wenda and Bran had waited so long that they hardly believed the time had come. But they shook their heads and did their bit, while Rees hauled in the anchor and looped the rope to the side of the boat.

And unbelievably, we came up off the hillside and stood away into the air.

For a while we seemed to move really fast. Wenda and Bran turned from normal-size people, waving us good-bye, to tiny distant dolls in no time at all. We went up and up and were in a golden dawn sky next moment, with sharp mountains beneath us; then we were high, high above green hillside reaching into wavy coastline outlined in white; after that we were over the sea. Rees allowed the boys to stop pumping, and they collapsed onto the creaking wickerwork sides. I hung on to a rope and stared back at a glorious view of Gallis as a misty crescent trailing into the distance to the south, all blue peaks and green or gold plains. Then it was too misty to see, and there was only water below. Sea from high up is oddly regular. I saw it as a grayness with white ripples crossing one another like the pattern of a plaid. It was very empty. I looked ahead and wondered where Logra was. There was nothing on the horizon but mist.

Riannan had been right. It was cold up there. Ivar

and Ogo wrapped themselves in their plaids. Everyone else except Finn and Aunt Beck put coats on. Finn said cheerfully that he was used to worse in Bernica. Aunt Beck pronounced that Skarr was much colder. We laughed. We were all surprisingly happy. Plug-Ugly lay on my feet and purred. Green Greet flapped himself to a rope, where he hung sideways, staring around. Blodred was even more enterprising. She scrambled over Rees's head onto another rope and went climbing out over the tight patchwork until we lost sight of her.

"Will she be all right?" Riannan asked anxiously.

"I hope so," said Rees, craning his head after her just as anxiously. "She's usually pretty sensible."

We must have sailed for an hour, apparently standing still in the air, until things started to go wrong.

Ogo said, "The sea seems very near."

He was right. When I looked down, I could see waves climbing and smashing in sprays of white. It was no longer possible to make out the neat plaid pattern. It was just gray, angry water to the far horizon.

Rees, who had been feeding another bag of charcoal onto the fire, jumped up and looked. "Gallis! We're far too low! Ivar, Ogo, start pumping." He hurriedly hitched two more wooden treadles to the bellows and began treading away at one furiously.

"Will we sink?" Ivar asked as he climbed toward the nearest treadle.

"Shouldn't do," Rees said. "Not with the wheelless cart underneath. Finn, would you pump, too, please?"

The four of them began treadling hard, puffing and red in their faces. The fire roared and made its change from bluish to red and then to yellow-white. And the sea still came nearer. Shortly I could hear the waves crashing. Salty spray came aboard and spattered our faces. Aunt Beck calmly licked her lips, but I panicked.

"Rees, we're right down!" I yelled. A spout of water came aboard and hissed on the fire.

"Damnation of the gods!" Rees panted. "I think the wheelless spell's run out. Riannan, start singing the spell. Sing for your life!"

Riannan stood up, holding on to one of the ropes, and sang, lovely clean notes and strange words. It was a tune I knew from Skarr. It made your heart lift, that song, but it did nothing for the balloon. We came so low that the wicker boat began pitching and tossing like a real boat. Foamy water swirled up through the chinks.

"*Everyone* sing!" Rees gasped, still pumping. "Come on! All of you!"

He began to sing too, in gasps, the same song. Finn, Ivar, and Ogo joined in, in jerks. Finn knew one set of words, Ivar and Ogo another, and they all roared them out regardless, song of Skarr muddled with words of Bernica. Green Greet flapped down onto Finn's heaving shoulders and seemed to be croaking out the song too.

I looked down and met Plug-Ugly's wide, accusing eyes. He thought I should sing, too. "But you must know I can't sing!" I wailed.

He went on looking, the way only a cat can.

"All right," I said. "All *right*!" And I did the only thing

I could think of, which was to intone the "Hymn of the Wise Women." The words of it had never made sense to me. Aunt Beck had once confessed that she couldn't understand them either. But I boomed them out.

> "I am the salmon leaping the fall,
> I am the thunder of the bull that gores,"

I boomed, all on one note.

"Ha galla ferrin magonellanebry!" Riannan's sweet voice caroled.

"The sun spearing the lake is me," I boomed grimly on. "I am the note of the bird."

"And let the soft rain fall on me!" Finn roared, pumping.

"We men of Skarr shall triumph all the way!" Ivar and Ogo yelled, pumping, too.

"Verily the cunning of the cat is in me," I persevered.

"Ha galla fenin hiraya delbar," Rees sang along with Riannan.

We must have sounded like the maddest choir ever assembled. I looked across at Aunt Beck and found she was chanting our Hymn too. She seemed not to notice she was being showered with spray as she did so.

"And the power of running is mine to claim,
The fire is in me that gives the dragon wings,
And this I will use when the purpose merits,
When the light needs to lance to the target
And the growth comes with the turn of the year . . ."

I had got so far when I noticed Riannan pointing upward, looking amazed as she sang. I looked up too and was so astonished that I nearly forgot to go on chanting. Beyond the large patchwork curve of the balloon I could see a great red wing beating, and if I leaned backward, I had just a glimpse of a long, whisking lizard tail. Blodred. That's Blodred!

I thought. She's grown huge. She's *helping*!

But it was an absolute rule that you did not stop chanting the Hymn once you had started, so I went on to

"When the moon changes from full to crescent . . ."

and as I chanted on, I saw Rees pause in his song, though not in his pumping, to point upward too. I think he said something like "I *knew* Blodred was special!" But the Hymn was not finished, so I went grimly on.

"I am the moon and the changes of the moon.
Indeed I am all things changing and living
And burn like a spark in the mind's eye."

As I chanted, I imagined seeing Blodred above us on top of the balloon, clutching the many-colored fabric with her lizardly hands and working her webbed wings to take us along. Rees had been wrong to say they were not really wings, I thought. They *were* wings. And

I thought the sea might be getting a little farther away.

But the others were still singing. And Aunt Beck, instead of stopping at the end of the Hymn, simply went back to the beginning again.

"I am the salmon leaping the fall . . ."

I hurriedly joined in. We went through the whole Hymn twice more before we were somehow hauling ourselves into the sky again and no longer being drenched with sea spray. Almost without our realizing it, we were up into dazzling sun. Out of the dazzle I could see a gray-blue misty hump. We were nearly at Logra, it seemed. And we were going higher and higher yet.

"Right, everyone," Rees said. "Stop now, phew!" He sat down on the wickerwork with a crunch.

And—I am fairly sure—we went on upward. My ears felt strange.

"Going deaf," Aunt Beck announced. "Ears cracking."

"Not really," Riannan said soothingly. "This happens on high mountains too. Your ears pop."

Now I could see a whole golden curve of landscape on the horizon. If I looked up, I could see a red slice of Blodred's left wing, flapping us steadily onward. Looking forward again, I could pick out a line of white foam where the barrier must be, although the barrier was of course invisible.

"What do we do," I said, "if the barrier turns out to be a dome over Logra and we can't get through?"

"Then we'll land on top of it and wait for evening," Rees said, "when the wind turns the other way. We'll just have to hope it doesn't blow us back to some part of Gallis where the priests can see us. We'd be in real trouble then."

"Would the priests *really* object to the balloon?" Ivar asked. "Gronn struck me as a very easygoing man."

Finn chuckled a little. "Then you don't know priests, lad."

"The very *least* that would happen," Rees said, "was

that we would all be put in prison for years, while they decided exactly how unholy we've been."

To my surprise, this seemed to register with Aunt Beck. "*Now* he tells us!" she said.

Rees looked a little rueful. "I wanted you all to come," he said.

"And we have," I said. It surprises me now that even *then* I didn't realize what little planning we had done and how we all seemed to think it was going to be easy once we got to Logra. Everyone was staring forward at the steadily growing curve of land. It was coming up fast, but I still couldn't tell if the barrier covered it or not.

Soon we were above the white line of surf. It was obvious the breakers were huge. The wind must have been really strong. There was a gap of calm sea, and then we were rushing across what ought to have been land. But it was a marshy mix of mud and water. I thought I saw submerged houses and then a straggling of tents where the people from the houses seemed to be camping out.

"You know," Rees said, "it looks as if the barrier has made the rivers back up into floods."

We had no time to consider this. A great wind suddenly sprang up. It hit me in the back like a hard hand, and I know I yelped. Finn grabbed Green Greet to him by the tips of his one hand. Then we were riding with the wind, speeding over swollen rivers and lakes with trees standing out of them, then over inundated fields, winding roads, villages, and a small town. I saw Blodred's wing retreat to the top of the balloon. Shortly she came sliding down a rope to Rees's shoulder, a small lizard again. And still we hurtled on.

Logra is enormous. It is by far the largest of the islands. We rushed across it, over field after field, village after town, for a good hour, to judge by the steadily climbing sun, and the other coast of it was still not in sight. At first I thought the place was even flatter than Bernica; but we drifted lower as we went, and then I could see that there were plenty of hills and valleys, just lower than I was used to and all seeming splendidly fertile. Now we could see people on the roads, riding horses or walking. Most of them were looking up at us and pointing. Others ran out of houses to look and point too.

"I wish I could have made us invisible," Rees said uneasily.

"We're attracting a lot of notice," Finn agreed.

"I think we should go higher," Rees said. "Everyone to the pumps again."

So we all crowded to the bellows, except Aunt Beck, and became too hot and breathless for a while to see if people were seeing us or not. When I did get a chance to look, we were high, high again and passing over some quite large towns.

"I don't think the barrier *is* a dome," I said. "There must be thousands of people down there. Surely they would have run out of air after ten years."

"We must give thought to where we need to land," Finn suggested.

"Need to land," Green Greet said.

"I was hoping we could come down somewhere near whatsis. The capital city," Rees said. "It's nearly opposite the Pandy. What's its name again?"

"Haranded," Riannan and Ogo said together.

This made me realize that Ogo had hardly said a word for hours. I looked at him, and I could see he was full of strange feelings.

"Do you remember any of this?" I asked him.

"Not really," he said. "Just the colors. The towns are red, and the fields are yellow and green. And there's a smell coming up that I know." He pulled his lips in hard against his teeth, and I could see he was struggling not to cry. I knew better than to make him talk anymore.

I considered the smell. Logra smelled of hay and spices and smoke. Gallis had smelled of heather and incense, Bernica of damp farmyards. I remembered, like biting on a sore tooth, the scents of Skarr—stone, lichen, gorse, and bracken—and I felt like crying too, for a moment.

Meanwhile the others were arguing about how we were to recognize Haranded if we came to it.

"It must be a big city," Rees said. "We can damp down the fire when we see it—no problem there."

"It would be simpler to take the spell off the raft," Riannan said.

"But we have to be sure where we are," Rees insisted.

"Won't there be large buildings?" Finn said.

"Yes, fine large ones. It'll be where the King lives," Ivar said. "But we just went over a place with a golden dome. Have we overshot?"

Here Ogo conquered his emotions and said, very definitely, "The King's palace is on a hill in the middle of Haranded. It's white. It has big towers with blue roofs."

Everyone relaxed a little at this. Rees said, "Warn me when you see it. We don't want to land on its roof."

Nothing like that happened. We had time to eat our provisions, and Rees was beginning to watch our fuel anxiously and say he hoped we would have enough left to get us aloft again when we began to discern the outline of a large city, over to our left and a good many miles off.

"We're going to miss it," Ivar said. "We're miles to the south of it."

The words were scarcely out of his mouth when Plug-Ugly reared up beside me out of nowhere and threw himself hard against me. I went down with a wallop into the bottom of the boat. Winds hit us from all quarters as I fell. I lay on my back with Plug-Ugly crouching on my stomach and saw the fire streaming just above me, roaring. I would have been burned but for Plug-Ugly. Next second the fire was streaming another way. I had jumbled sights of all of us throwing ourselves flat and the balloon above us blatting this way, then that way. I could feel us lurching and spinning. The fire roared and bellied round in a stream, and I watched, feeling it inevitable, as the flames bit into the great silken patchwork and set it burning over our heads.

Rees howled out the words of a quenching spell. Riannan broke into song. The flames went out in gusts of beastly-smelling smoke, but the damage was done. With a third of the great balloon missing, we went down and sideways. I could feel us doing it. When I scrambled to my knees and looked over the side, I could see the ground rushing underneath us and ourselves no higher than a house. I was truly terrified.

But the winds had left us by then. We slowed, and slowed more, and went down until we skimmed hedges. I saw a horseman duck as we sailed over him. I saw the city that had seemed so far off now only a mile or so away. I saw Rees standing up, swinging the anchor on its rope and Finn beside him, bleeding from one arm, where Green Greet had frantically clung on to him.

"That field there," Finn said. "There's no one to get hurt there."

We missed the field. We came down in a road with a mighty grinding and a whoosh as the hot air left the silk and the burned patchwork flopped down half across us.

Next moment we were surrounded by people. "Kill them!" they yelled. "Kill them! They put that damned barrier up!"

⌒ XIII ⌒

Logra people are taller than I was used to, and fairer, and they have a strange accent. A whole crowd of tall, skinny, ragged women were pulling at the balloon, shrieking. It took me a moment to gather that they were yelling, "It's silk! It's real silk! What a waste of good clothing!"

The men, who were equally ragged and even taller, were rocking at the boat where we sat, trying to tip us out, but the spell on the floater kept pulling us back upright and defeating them. Ivar had his sword drawn and was shouting, "Keep off! Keep back! First one to touch us gets his throat cut!" Green Greet was flapping and shrieking. Rees and Ogo both had their knives out, and Plug-Ugly was rearing up, spitting. This made the people hesitate to touch us, but I knew it was only a matter of time before someone got brave enough to climb aboard. Then we would be swamped.

What fools we've been! I thought. None of us had made any kind of plan about what we would do once we got here. It was as if we all had thought that just getting to Logra would be enough. Here somebody seized hold of Aunt Beck where she sat in the front. I scrambled over, shouting, "Don't you *dare*!" in a booming voice I didn't know I had. The person let go hurriedly.

It wasn't because of my voice. Horsemen were galloping up, surrounding the crowd. They had swords out that were larger and wider than Ivar's, and they were hitting people with the flat of them. One of them called out in a loud, official voice, "Get back! Leave the prisoners to us!" They all wore some sort of uniform — soldiers, I supposed.

"Are we rescued?" Ivar said.

"I doubt it," Rees said, but Ivar sheathed his sword anyway.

We were definitely prisoners. The soldiers wouldn't speak to us, except to say, "None of you move." Some of them cut the charred patchwork loose from the boat. Others brought up more horses—rather elderly, skinny horses that must have belonged to the ragged people, to judge by the yells of protest—and hitched a whole row of them to the boat. Then someone cracked a whip, and we were towed off in a grim crowd of riders. We could only look at one another and shrug.

Haranded was barely a mile away. There were no walls. Houses just grew larger and more frequent around us and became crooked streets with shops to either side. I liked the houses, nervous though I was. They were all built of brick with red roofs, in hundreds of fancy patterns. People were busy rolling aside shutters over the shops, then pausing to stare at us. I was surprised to see it was still early in the morning for these people.

I felt as if we had lived through most of a day already.

Presently we came into a wide street leading uphill. It had statues on each side, mostly very big, of men and women in flowing robes.

"What a very boastful road," I whispered to Ogo. "Who are all the statues?"

"Kings, queens, wizards—maybe some gods," Ogo answered. "I *think* it was called Royal Avenue."

He must have been right because the street led straight up to the white walls of the palace, where there was a big gate. More men in uniform were waiting for us there. The leader of the horsemen said to the one with gold on his coat, "The spies from the flying machine, sir."

"Good," said Gold-coat. And he said to one of his soldiers, "Go and tell the magistrate. He must be awake by now."

The soldier said, "Yessir," and went off through the gate at a run.

I realized, as we were towed through the gate into a

square courtyard, that they must have been able to see us in the air for miles and had made ready for us.

The gate clanged shut behind us, and more lowly-looking people hurried out to take the horses away. They wanted to take Green Greet away too, but Finn shouted, "No, no, this is the Guardian of the West! He stays with me!" while Green Greet flew shrieking into the air, alarming them all. They left him alone then, and he sat on Finn's shoulder again. Plug-Ugly was invisible. I realized that he had vanished as soon as the horsemen arrived. And of course no one saw Blodred, hiding up Rees's sleeve. So all ten of us were together as we were made to climb out of the boat and march into the great white building ahead.

Aunt Beck made quite a nuisance of herself. At first she wouldn't climb out of the boat, and when they tried pulling her, she shouted, "Take your hands off me! How dare you touch a Wise Woman of Skarr!" Everyone hastily let go of her and Gold-coat said, "Madam, if you don't get out by yourself, I shall personally carry you!"

While this was going on, I said despairingly to Rees, "What do we do now?"

Rees was looking quite unreasonably calm, to my mind. "Something will happen," he said. "Just be patient."

Meanwhile, Aunt Beck climbed out onto the flagstones with great dignity. Then we were marched off into the palace.

Logra people were certainly not early risers. By the time we had clattered through some very unimpressive wooden corridors and been herded into a bare wooden room, the magistrate was only just arriving, still struggling into his white official robes and yawning as he sat on the only chair in the place. He was a shaggy, stupid-looking man, as unimpressive as the room. About the only impressive thing there was a giant picture painted on the plaster wall of a bull with large blue wings. As the magistrate fussily settled himself, I pointed at it and asked Ogo, "Whatever is *that*?"

Gold-coat answered me, sounding shocked, "That

is the image of the Great Guardian of Logra. Show respect, young woman."

"I need to go to the toilet," Aunt Beck announced.

"Show them where," the magistrate said wearily. "Show them all."

So we were led off again. Riannan, Aunt Beck, and I were shown to a fairly well-appointed whitewashed place with a privy in it. I must say it was very welcome. I imagine the others felt the same. At any rate, Finn, Ivar, Ogo, and Rees were herded back into the room looking a good deal more cheerful.

"Now," the magistrate said, "can we begin, please?" He had been given a steaming cup of something while we were gone, and he sipped at it, glowering at us over the top of it. "I must say you are a very motley lot of spies."

"We are *not* spies," Ivar said, glowering back.

"Then why are you here?" said the magistrate. "And you address me as Your Honor."

Rees took hold of Ivar's arm to shut him up.

"Because," he said, "er, Your Honor, I had the notion that the barrier could be crossed from the air and we wished to prove it. As you see, we did prove it."

"A very inadequate story," the magistrate said. "Of course you came to spy. What puzzles me is why there are seven of you from all over the place."

Gold-coat said, pointing at Aunt Beck, "This one claims to be a Wise Woman of Skarr, Your Honor."

The magistrate looked at Aunt Beck, with her hair half undone because of the winds. "Well, I've heard they're all wild mad females. She could be. It makes no difference to my decision. They're all foreigners. Lock them all up until the Regent has time to deal with them."

"Regent?" said Aunt Beck. "What Regent is this? I thought you had a king."

"The Regent is the King's brother, who rules because of the King's illness," the magistrate said. "And you address me as Your Honor."

"Then you address *me* as Wisdom," Aunt Beck said.

"No, I don't," said the magistrate. "You're a spy. Lock them all up."

"But I'm a Prince of Skarr," Ivar protested. "I shouldn't be locked up."

"Nor should my sister be," Rees said. "She's a starred singer of Gallis."

"Address me as Your Honor!" the magistrate almost screamed.

"And I am a holy monk from Bernica," Finn added. "To lock me up is ungodly."

"Say Your *Honor*!" the magistrate yelled.

Ogo, rather hesitantly, stepped forward and said, "Your Honor, I am a citizen of Logra. I was born here and—"

The magistrate looked at him scornfully. "Oh, yes? You come here wearing barbaric Skarr clothing and tell me that! You're obviously one of the great tall savages they breed there."

Ogo's face was pink. He was, I saw, taller than anyone else in the room. He must have been growing madly lately. He started to speak, and the magistrate cut in with "Now you're going to bleat at me that you're really a prince, like that boy there." He pointed to Ivar.

Ivar said, "But I *am!*"

Ogo began. "Well—"

"Oh, take them *away!*" the magistrate howled. "Lock them up with the other prisoners until the Regent has time to deal with them." He dumped his mug on the side of his chair and waved both arms with his hands flopping. The cup keeled over and crashed to the floor. "Now look what you've made me do!" he said.

I found it hard not to laugh, in spite of the trouble we were in. Riannan *was* laughing, with one hand over her mouth. But Ivar was seething. Ogo was breathing heavily and looked to be near tears. As the soldiers shoved us out of the room, Ivar took his feelings out on Ogo by saying, "Don't worry. *We* all know you're the Ogre from Logra."

Rees expressed *his* feelings by saying, "What a very low grade of official. Can't they afford anyone better?

If that man was a priest in Gallis, he'd be serving in Synon."

"Or in Gorse End," Riannan agreed.

"Are those very low places?" I asked. "I do hope so."

Aunt Beck startled me by saying, "He should be mucking out cattle."

Gold-coat and the other soldiers made no objection to any of this. I had the feeling that they agreed with us, but the reason they said nothing may have been that we began going upstairs then, long wooden stairs. The soldiers panted and did not seem to enjoy this. We were all so used to walking up hills that we found the climb no trouble at all. We went down a corridor and then up long stone stairs, and Rees talked all the way, describing Synon and then Gorse End and exactly what miserable places they both were. I told him I was relieved to find there were parts of Gallis that were *not* idyllically beautiful.

"Oh, yes," he said as we began on another stone flight, "there are parts of Gallis that no bard will visit, so they get worse all the time."

By this time we had climbed so many stairs that I was expecting us to be imprisoned in a high tower. I was quite surprised when we wheeled aside and clattered through a big anteroom that smelled rather deliciously of warm wood. Logra, I was beginning to see, was hotter than any country I had yet been in. It must by then have been midmorning, and the sun blazed in through a dozen tall windows.

Beyond the anteroom we marched into a dark corridor running left to right. There was a whole row of doors there, all locked and bolted. We were made to stop by the nearest door, which had more bolts to it than any of the others. While we were standing waiting for a soldier to draw all the bolts back, I could have sworn that someone came out through a bolted door far to the left and dodged hastily back on seeing us.

Then the door was flung open on a big, well-lighted space. The soldiers pushed us forward while Gold-coat called out, "Some friends to see you, Prince."

We stood in a huddle, staring at a huge hall with

a row of empty arches opposite to us open to the sky and at the small crowd of people scattered about in it. Prince Alasdair was the first one I saw. He was pale as a ghost, lying on a sofa near the middle of the place. There were crusty, bloodstained bandages over his legs, one of them yellow with infection. It looked horrible. I knew he had been wounded, but not how badly.

He stared at us, and so did the crowd of his followers. They were all wearing the hunting gear they had been captured in, very threadbare now, but quite clean. Everyone stared for the long minute it took the soldiers to bolt the door outside, and then for the longer minute when they could be heard marching away.

Then everyone came to life.

"Finn, you old devil!" someone shouted. "You've brought us the green bird!" At which Green Greet took off from Finn's shoulder and flew from man to man, uttering whooping squawks. Finn began to laugh.

Prince Alasdair fetched a cloth up from beside his couch and briskly rubbed his face with it. His head was for a moment in a cloud of white powder. Then he threw down the cloth, carefully pulled his legs out from the horrible bandages, and leaped to his feet. And there he strode toward us perfectly well, with his face a healthy color, though I could see the carefully mended rip in his trews where he had been wounded.

"Beck!" he cried out. "Beck, by all the gods—"

To my extreme astonishment, my aunt ran to meet him, and they embraced like lovers, she saying, "Oh, Allie, I thought my heart was broken when they took you!" and Prince Alasdair simply saying, "My love, my love!"

Well, well! I thought. I'd had no idea Aunt Beck had been carrying a broken heart all this time. I hadn't even known that she and Prince Alasdair knew each other. But there she was, not only restored to her usual self but looking years younger, with her face all rosy and delighted and her hair still wild from the wind. It occurred to me that *this* was why Aunt Beck had not refused outright to go on this rescue—which I knew, when I thought about it, that she was quite capable of—and why she had kept going when we were landed in Bernica with no money. Well, well.

By this time all the other prisoners had crowded round us, so I pulled myself together and made introductions. It was clear that Finn needed none. Ossen, the courtier who had shouted to Finn, very quickly drew him aside to a seat by the open archways, where he produced a stone bottle and a couple of big mugs. I feared that before the morning was out Finn would be quite disgracefully drunk! I introduced Ivar instead. Someone said, "My cousin Mevenne's son?" and Ivar was pulled aside to give news of the family almost at once.

I introduced Ogo next. I felt he deserved some attention. I explained how he had been left behind in Skarr. Prince Alasdair said, with his arm round Aunt Beck, "Have you told them you are a man of Logra, lad?"

Ogo said wryly, "I tried."

"I'll sort it out for you," Alasdair promised. "Never fear."

"And these," I said, "are Rees and Riannan from the

Pandy in Gallis. It was Rees's invention that brought us here."

"The Pandy?" said someone. A fine big man with a most noble beard pushed his way toward them. "Bran's children?" He was wearing faded bardic blue. It dawned on me that he must be my father. I was overcome with shyness and decided to keep my mouth shut from then on.

Aunt Beck put a stop to the eager explanations about the balloon and how Bran had started it by inventing the floating sledges when she pointed at me. "*She's* the one you should be asking after, Gareth. She's your own daughter."

"What, Aileen?" my father said, staring at me. "But she was a tiny child!"

"She's had time to grow up," said my aunt, "and become a Wise Woman."

I could see my father could think of nothing to say. After a while he said cautiously, "And your mother, Aileen?"

"Dead," said Aunt Beck, and she shot a look at me to warn me to say nothing of the Priest of Kilcannon. As if I would have done. I was as tongue-tied as my father, but I supposed we would manage to talk to each other when everyone had finished telling of our adventures.

But there seemed to be no time for that. Prince Alasdair said, "Rory, you had better go now and get that fruit Lucella promised us. And say we need some wine too. You can tell her why."

The man who nodded and went off was, I was sure, the same man I had glimpsed dodging back through the locked door earlier. This time he went to a different door, which opened quite as easily.

"They're all unlocked," my father said, seeing me staring, "except the one we came in by. We're taking part in a farce here."

"Which we'd better get on with," Prince Alasdair said. "The Ministers will be here any minute now." He went to his couch and climbed nimbly back into the dreadful bandages. One of the other prisoners brought him a large box of powder, which Alasdair applied to his face with a bundle of feathers. In seconds he was a pale wounded invalid once more. "You new arrivals had better sit about looking gloomy, being upset at being taken prisoner, you know."

None of us knew what to make of this, but we spread about the great room, doing our best to look miserable. Ivar, Riannan, and Rees sat together on the floor, cross-legged and mournful. Aunt Beck went and sat next to Finn, where she eyed him until he guiltily hid his mug under the seat. Green Greet settled droopingly on the back of Finn's chair. Ogo and I, with natural curiosity, went over to the archways to see what was beyond.

Nothing was beyond, except a terrace with a few chairs on it. There was a low fence at the edge of the terrace and, beyond that, a huge drop down to the courtyard where we had come in. From our height it looked as small as this page of paper. The place did make a perfect prison. A spacious, airy, perfect prison. Once all the doors were locked, of course.

My father had come over there with us. He still seemed embarrassed. Ogo said to him, "I suppose you're all secretly busy making ropes?"

My father laughed. "We could be. But what good would it do? We could get to the ground easily enough, one way or another, but we'd still be in Logra, behind the barrier."

While he was speaking, there seemed to be a low, growing roar coming from the city beyond the courtyard. We saw the courtyard gates slam open, and two horses galloped in and stopped as if they could go no further. Even from up here, I could see that the beasts were covered with foam. The men on their backs, who were both wearing some sort of flapping purple robes, flung themselves off the horses and staggered, obviously as tired as the horses. People ran from the gates and the buildings around, shouting excitedly. Meanwhile the roar from the city grew and grew.

"I wonder what's going on," my father said. "Those look like—"

He was interrupted by a green whirr. Green Greet shot out of the archway right beside my ear and plunged out over the fence.

"—wizards," my father finished, leaning over to watch Green Greet plummet until he was a tiny green blur, then spread his wings and sail this way and that around the courtyard. "Does he do that often?"

"No," I said. "He's rather a sober bird, really."

The tired wizards were being helped into the palace by an eager crowd now. When they were out of sight, my father turned back into the wide prison, saying, "Best get into our act, then." And sighed.

And Green Greet was there again, soaring over the terrace on wide wings. "The barrier is down!" he screamed. "The barrier is down!"

"Perhaps," Ogo suggested, "we ought to start making ropes now."

ᔕ XIV ᔕ

Green Greet had barely landed back on Finn's shoulder when there was a rattle of bolts at the locked door. It was a useful noise. We had time to sit on the floor in suitably doleful attitudes. But Aunt Beck simply stayed where she was, sitting very upright beside Finn and looking every inch her usual self. In fact, I think she looked better than she ever had. She had color in her face and a near smile.

The door was flung open, and soldiers marched in, followed by Gold-coat, who announced menacingly, "The Regent's Ministers to interview the Prince. Show respect."

Show respect? Why? I wondered, as a group of lavishly dressed fellows followed Gold-coat into the room. There were pasty, pompous ones, small, weasely ones and large, loutish ones, and a couple who were plain ordinary. And I could see at a glance that every one of them was an empty-headed fool. They looked majestically around, and the soldiers hurried to bring them chairs so that they could sit face-to-face with Prince Alasdair. While they were arranging themselves, one of the doors farther along—one of those that looked locked but obviously wasn't—came open, and the man who had been sent to ask about fruit put his head around it. He saw the Ministers and dodged hurriedly out again.

"We have passed the laws you advised us to pass," a pasty, pompous Minister announced, "but we have yet to see any benefit from them."

"Well, such things do take time," Prince Alasdair said in a weak, ill voice.

"You mustn't tax the Prince's strength," Aunt Beck

said severely. "When did you pass these laws?"

They stared at her, much as people stared at Green Greet when he talked sense. My father said, melodious and bardic, "This lady is a Wise Woman of Skarr. Please attend to her every word."

"Oh," said the Minister. "Well. We passed the laws yesterday, Madam."

"Then it's no wonder nothing's happened yet," said my aunt. "You'll need to give it at least a month."

"Yes, Madam," they said.

One of the small, wispy ones began fluting away then, something about bylaws in the city, and I became too bored to listen. Instead I thought about how suddenly and mysteriously the barrier had come down. Perhaps all it needed was for someone from outside Logra to cross it. Had it come down as soon as our balloon went over? Those wizards, or whoever they were, had plainly ridden from a long way off, perhaps from the coast, traveling much more slowly than our balloon. And I remembered then the sudden strange gust of wind that had hit us as we crossed into Logra. That must have been the force of the barrier going down. Then, later, when those other gusts had hit us, those must have been from other parts of the barrier, the forces rushing inland to converge on where we flew. I thought we had been very lucky to survive those.

Thinking this way, I missed a great deal of droning talk. When I started hearing it again, Prince Alasdair was saying in his weak, invalid voice, "This is purely because the price of food is so high. Did I not tell you to make the merchants give up their stockpiles to the government? I know their barns are stuffed with corn."

"But the merchants would be so *angry* if we did that," a Minister quavered.

"Reassure them." Prince Alasdair sighed. "Now that the irrigation canals we designed for you are finished and working, next year should be a bumper crop. They can make huge profits then—and you can tax them, of course, so that—"

The locked door opened with a slam. A man in

official-looking robes pushed past the soldiers guarding it and hurried up to the pompous Minister. He bent and whispered urgently into the Minister's ear. The Minister jumped to his feet, saying, "Is this time. Then—" He beckoned furiously to the other Ministers. "Something has come up," he said. "We must leave you, Prince."

They all went rushing, helter-skelter, out through the door, and the soldiers went rushing out after them.

"Ah," said my father. He sat in one of the ring of empty chairs, grinning. "They've just heard that the barrier is down? Right?"

"And they'll find plenty of new problems to worry about," Prince Alasdair said, stretching his arms happily. He worked his feet out of the bandages, saying, "There have been droughts and flooding and near civil war in Logra since the barrier went up and Regent Waldo started ruling. Waldo is so *bad* at ruling. I honestly don't know what they'd have done without our advice."

"So you secretly govern Logra, do you?" my aunt

said. Prince Alasdair nodded, and grinned at her like a naughty boy. "And," asked my aunt, "how do you come to know about irrigation canals? There has never been any such thing in Skarr."

"Naturally not," the Prince said. "It rains in Skarr. I know about canals because I went to the palace library and read about them."

"How?" asked Aunt Beck.

"I borrowed a wizard's gown, and nobody looked at me twice," he said. "*Someone* had to do something about the poor people here. Waldo's notion is just to execute anyone who disagrees with him, which, you must admit, doesn't get anything useful done."

"True," said my aunt. "And then you seemed so certain that the work you ordered had been done. Did you *see* them build your canals?"

Prince Alasdair nodded. "We all did. Ossen got us horses and Gareth borrowed a whole bundle of wizard's gowns and we rode out almost daily to keep the men up to their work. Paying them was difficult, though.

Gareth and I had to raid Regent Waldo's treasury more than once."

My father coughed. "I sang the guards to sleep, naturally. No one was hurt."

My aunt said, almost indignantly, "So when I thought of you lying wounded in prison, it was no such thing."

"The wound did take a while to heal," the Prince admitted. "Long enough for me to discover how useful it was."

By this time we were all starting to laugh. Ogo whispered to me, "This is the most enterprising Prince I ever imagined. Do you think he'd have me as a courtier?"

"Why don't you ask?" I said.

As I said it, doors opened all along the room. People came in by the dozen, carrying bowls of fruit, trays of little loaves, and big platters of meat. Some of them had bottles of wine, others glasses and plates, and others again brought chairs, trestles, and boards, all of which they most quickly and efficiently assembled into a table with a feast on it.

"Wow," said Ivar.

"Courtesy of the palace stewardess," my father said. "Here she comes, the lovely Lucella."

A most striking little lady followed the busy servants in. She was very dark, in both her hair and her skin, and her face had a high-nosed sort of beauty I had never seen before. She was most demurely dressed in white satin with a blue stripe in it, which, although it was obviously a uniform, seemed to make her even more beautiful. My father later told me that she was Roven, from south Logra, where everyone looked like this. Whatever, it was very clear to me that my father was at least half in love with her. Why *is* it, I thought resentfully, that everyone I'm fond of seems to love someone else? But Lucella was so charming that I found it hard to blame my father.

She said, "Please forgive the delay. We had to wait for the Ministers to leave you. But"—she took up her striped apron and twisted it hesitantly—"but I really came because one of the prisoners claimed to be a native of Logra."

"Me," said Ogo. He was staring at her. "I was born here, but my uncle left me behind in Skarr."

Lucella was staring at Ogo as hard as he was staring at her. She said, "Can you be—"

Ogo said, "Are you Luci? My nurse was Luci."

And she cried out, "Oh, you are, you *are*! You're my little Hugo!" She rushed to Ogo and flung her arms around as much of him as she could reach. He towered over her. He had to bend down to hug her.

Hugo, I thought. Of course his name was really Hugo. It was just his Logra accent that made us all think it was Ogo. They do drop their aitches terribly.

Lucella kept hold of Ogo and stood back from him, beaming. Ogo was beaming even more broadly. "You used to sing to me and tell me the most wonderful stories," he said.

"I loved you as my own," Lucella said. "My, you've

grown big!" Then she turned to Prince Alasdair and said, very seriously, "You must keep this from Regent Waldo. He'll kill him if he knows." Everyone stopped smiling at once, but I nearly laughed at the appalled look on Ivar's face when she went on. "You see, Hugo is the king's son."

Next thing, I felt Plug-Ugly push against me so hard that I fell over just as a great wind lashed through the room. It smashed the feast on the tables, hurling jugs and bottles into the air and swirling people, like dummies, out of the row of doors that were slamming open and shut. It swept me across the floor the opposite way with a blast that threw me out onto the terrace and nearly took me over the edge. I heard my father's voice sing a great pure note, and the wind seemed to quail at the sound. It saved me because it gave me time to hang on to the fence. But when I looked back, everyone had gone. The room was empty except for furniture flying about and dashing itself against the walls.

Then I saw Ogo clinging to the handle of one of the

doors that was smacking open and shut as if it would shake him off. "Ogo!" I shouted. The wind filled my mouth and dried up the words in my throat. It was howling now too, so it drowned out my voice. But he heard me. I saw him nod. I crawled toward him, fighting the wind. It was so strong and so hard to move that I felt as if my hands and knees were glued to the floor. Airborne grapes, figs, and plums whistled over my head, and I had to keep ducking. I'd nearly reached Ogo when Prince Alasdair's sofa hurtled, end-on, toward me with shoals of little loaves whisking round it. I threw myself flat and felt it skim my hair before I heard it lam into the arches behind me and fall to pieces; then on I crawled, with the wind screaming in my ears. Ogo wedged his shoulder in the door, and it closed on him like a vise, trying to squeeze him out of the room. It must have hurt a lot, but he stayed put long enough for me to crawl through the gap, past his legs and into the corridor. Then he was heaved out onto the floor beyond me, and the door clapped shut. Bolts shot; keys turned. Did it think it had locked us in, or out?

We sat on the floor, panting with effort, and I managed to gasp out a thank-you to him for rescuing me. The thought that I could have been locked in the room with that killer wind was frightening. I was fairly sure it was the same wind as the gusting one that had set light to our balloon. It was obvious now that it had been sent to do it on purpose. And I guessed that the wind that had carried us across Logra had been conjured, too. It hadn't been caused by the barrier coming down, as I'd thought, and it hadn't blown us toward the capital by chance. It had intended to bring us here. I started to say so, and Ogo just nodded again. He'd already worked that out. We could hear it still beating about on the other side of the doors. Then we heard it stop. We heard the crash of furniture and tinkle of cutlery as broken bits of things fell back to the floor. Then there was silence. There was a kind of fury to that silence. "It's realized it hasn't got us," I whispered. "Run!"

We ran for our lives down endless corridors and

staircases. We didn't know where we were going or where the others had been taken; we just ran. I was afraid the clatter of our feet on the wooden steps would give us away, but the wind appeared to have lost us or given up. I almost laughed at Ogo running beside me. The wind had flung a pie into his hair, and he was spotted with pastry flakes. He didn't look much of a prince. He saw me smile and took my hand and, I have to say, we went twice as fast with his long legs at full stretch.

We both saw the feather at the same time. It was on the floor ahead of us: one of Green Greet's green feathers lying outside a hefty wooden door. "They must all have been blown this way through the door," Ogo panted.

I think I was expecting to find them all there, on the other side, in another magistrate's room or even a dungeon. Instead we found ourselves alone in a beautiful little paved court, enclosed by the white palace walls. A few windows overlooked it, but they were tightly shuttered. In the center was a long oblong of rippling water with cypress trees stationed at each corner, like dark pencils. There was a fountain of sorts at the far end—a tall, sculpted block of stone—that fed a peaceful-sounding cascade into the rippling water. It was so unexpectedly calm, and we were so breathless and frightened and pastry covered that I felt like an intruder in a sacred place. I think Ogo felt the same because he turned to go back. Then a streak of sunlight on the surface caught my eye. "Bless me!" I panted. "There's another of Green Greet's feathers." The sun had lit it up, floating and rocking at the base of the falling water.

We ran along the water's edge and looked across at the feather bobbing about under the fountain, which towered over us—a lovely intertwining of running, lithe creatures. Higher up, there were giant sea horses supporting the figures of a bird, a dragon, a great cat, and a winged bull—the four Guardians of our world. The water poured down out of the gaping mouth of a huge fish they were all holding. But the feather, pitching about down at the bottom, was not at all bedraggled by the splashes, which was odd. "What's it doing there?" Ogo asked. I didn't know. We walked round behind the fountain, as if there could be an answer there. But there wasn't, and we trailed back to the front. I was getting very worried now about Aunt Beck and my father and all the others. I was miserable too, because I was beginning to think we might never find them.

A pressure at the back of my legs and sinewy winding round my knees cheered me up at once. "Oh, Plug-Ugly," I cried, "I thought that terrible wind had got you!" A throbbing, purring spit, a "Fat chance!" sort of spit, came by way of an answer. And I suddenly felt much safer. "He seems to want us to paddle," I told Ogo as Plug-Ugly gave me a little push toward the water's edge.

Ogo jumped in and then helped me down. The water only came just over his ankles, but I was up to my shins. We waded over to the feather, and Ogo put it in his belt. He had four now. But what were we supposed to do next? It was puzzling. We looked back along the rippling water. "They can't all have been blown here," Ogo said. "There would be more signs of them." He grinned. "Like the fruit jelly all over the back of your dress." How he could laugh when we were in such trouble defeats me. I nearly reminded him that the Regent would kill him if he knew he was here. Instead I told him crossly he'd be as well to sluice his great pastry head under the fountain. "Yuk," he said as soon as he felt his hair, and did.

"Shush," I told him as he shouted with the freezing cold of it.

He looked up at the huge fish reproachfully. "You'd think a salmon your size could do us the favor of warming up the water."

"How do you know it's a salmon?" I asked, but I wasn't really wanting an answer because what he'd said had jerked at something at the back of my mind and made me think about the feathers differently. What if they hadn't fallen by chance? Might Green Greet have left them there deliberately? I looked up at the water cascading from the fish's mouth, like a small waterfall. "I think these feathers are directions," I said. "Green Greet is showing us the way." He stared at me.

"The way to what?"

"How should I know?" I sighed. "I'm only a Wise Woman—a learner one, at that. But I'm going to climb the waterfall. Give me a leg up." And he helped me clamber up onto a running hare.

It was a slippery climb to the top—about three times the height of Ogo. The fountain may have *looked* beautiful, but everything was covered in thick water-washed slime. It was a bit like climbing a mountain of frog spawn. The water kept hitting me slaps on the top of my head, but I suppose it got rid of the fruit jelly. I pulled myself up by stone tails and manes, hooves and antlers. At the top, I wrapped one arm round the cat's neck and looked about. There was nothing but a different view of the same thing. What was I doing up here, soaked through and nothing to show for it?

I looked into the cat's face and—I no longer know if this is true—I could have sworn the sun glinted on its wet stone eyes and turned them the exact green-blue of Plug- Ugly's eyes, and they slewed to look behind me into the fish's great mouth. Beyond the water, running smooth as satin over its lip, were steps going down into darkness.

I waved at Ogo and gestured at the fish, to show him what I was doing; then I crawled into the mouth. I could nearly stand upright. The water piling over the edge took up most of the room in there. I had to squeeze past it along a narrow, slippery space at the side. I went slowly; it would be simple enough to be dragged over the edge with it. Once past, it was an easy climb down the steps. They spiraled down and down and down. I must have been far deeper than the height of the fountain, but I could see my way fairly well in the grayish dark. That should have been a warning. What kind of light could be here, so deep down?

Then such a strong, urgent longing for Skarr and home swept over me that I had to stand still for a minute and steady myself against the cold walls. I could smell the sea, the salty, seaweed-and-cockles tang of the sea that was never far from wherever you walk on Skarr. I shook myself free of the homesickness and went on down. I couldn't possibly have smelled the sea so far inland.

Quite soon after that, the steps ended. The light brightened so quickly that I was blinded for a minute and could scarcely see the cavernous room I was standing in with a man sitting in the middle of it. For a mad moment I thought it was Ogo. There was a hint of Ogo in his face. But then I saw he was much older than Ogo, and worse, I saw his weird, pulsing aura that was like a halo of poison. He reminded me of something. Was it a jellyfish? No. He was like a sponge—a seeking, searching sponge—that sucked up everything it needed. "Hello," he said in a soft voice that could smother your hopes.

But it wasn't him I was looking at anymore. There was a small calf lying on the rocky ground next to him, so cruelly tied and trussed up that I could hardly make out the shape of it at all. Broad, mustard-colored ribbons of seaweed lay across its barnacled back, but just visible through the tangle of dark magic binding it to the ground, were its small blue wings. It looked up at me, and I could see in its eyes a longing to die. I thought: Please, you mustn't do that. Then I saw something more terrible in that look. The calf knew that whatever it suffered, it *couldn't* die, and I guessed this tiny, helpless creature was the great Guardian of the East, the blue-winged bull. How had it come to such a state?

The man was smiling now. He wore splendid purple robes and a brilliant ring on every finger. As for his neck, there was enough gold hanging round it to win the envy of Ivar's brother, Donal. "Look what the wind has blown in," he said, just as softly, and I knew it was he who had sent the wind to kill us. The sickening energy that seeped out of his sucking presence scared me. He was powerful. I'd a suspicion that the wind he'd conjured was just child's play to him. I had never met such a powerful wizard in my life. "But we've met before, Aileen," he said, as if he'd read my thoughts. "On Skarr, at the conference you and your aunt had with the High King Farlane. Remember? At your cousin King Kenig's castle." I shook my head. How could he possibly have been at that meeting? I'd known everyone in the room. Except of course the High King's attendants behind his chair. Could he have been one of them? I'd hardly noticed them. True, the High King had said the Lograns could send spies through the barrier to Skarr. But even a wizard of this man's stature couldn't pass himself off as an attendant without someone realizing. I was certain of that.

He smiled even more broadly. "You look unconvinced, Aileen. Afterward I gave you a purse for your expenses. Remember?"

Who could forget that purse? It had turned out to be full of stones.

"Sorry about the stones," he said in his soft voice that didn't mean a word of it.

That scared me even more. There was no way he could have known about the stones unless he'd been the attendant at the meeting. It must have taken deep magic for him to stand there unnoticed. Even Aunt Beck hadn't seen through it. It was the sort of magic you'd be a fool to cross.

"Who are you?" I asked. I was surprised at the firm way it came out. Not giving away the frightened shaking inside me.

"I'm Waldo," he replied. "Regent Waldo."

There was the sound of hurrying footsteps behind me, and Ogo came into the huge room. "Are you all right?" he asked anxiously.

I said quickly to warn him, "Regent Waldo, this is Prince Ivar's servant, Ogo."

ꙮ XV ꙮ

Waldo told us everything we might have wanted to know. He told it so completely, we knew he didn't intend us to survive long enough to pass it on to anyone else. All the time he was talking, the calf trembled with cold—or that's what I thought it was, at first.

"You see, my dears," he said, as if he were telling little children a bedtime story, "we poor old Lograns had to stop the Chaldean Islands' warring with us. We were perilously close to defeat. I appealed to our great protector, the Lord of the East, the blue-winged bull, and with a little persuasion, he agreed we should make a barrier to keep you all at bay."

"What kind of persuasion would that be?" I asked.

"Why, we told him the truth," Waldo said innocently. "We Lograns were losing the war because the other three Guardians, of the West, South, and North, were helping Skarr, Bernica, and Gallis in the fight."

"There's not a whisker of truth in that," I said. Ogo gave me a kind of "be careful" nudge, meaning not to make him angry, but I couldn't help myself: I felt so sorry for the calf, and I went on, "It would take warped magic to convince a Guardian of such a thing." He pretended to be shocked.

"Aileen, child! How can you say that? I've heard this about you: suspicious to the point of insolence." He nearly caught me out, nearly sidetracked me by making me wonder who he'd heard it from and if I minded. But with a wizard of his strength I had to concentrate for every second if we were to try and get out of this alive.

It was Ogo who plowed on. "Did the King agree to making the barrier too?" he asked abruptly.

Waldo gave him a sharp look. "The King was losing the war."

"Don't you mean you were losing the war for him, on purpose?" I asked.

It was a guess, but I could tell I was right by the way Waldo wagged a jeweled finger at me and said, "What a spiteful thought, Aileen! Betray my own brother? No, the war was destroying Logra, and the King begged for my help. As his *loyal* brother"—he paused to give me a smile that would stop you wanting your food for a week, then went on—"I ended the war by making the barrier. But alas, the King became a sick man, too grief-stricken with the loss of his son to rule sensibly." He sighed—a truly disgusting sigh that he didn't even bother to make sound sincere—and added, "Reluctantly, I had to step in and take over." Ogo's mouth went into that straight line it makes when he is holding back words and feelings.

I said, "You must have been upset too. You're his son's uncle. You were in charge of him when he got left behind on Skarr, weren't you?"

"A dreadful tragedy!" Waldo was handling my question like oiled water. "The King said that we should only put up the barrier as a last resort, and he sent me to Skarr to make a final bid for peace. To my everlasting regret, I took the little Prince with me as a mark of our good faith." I swear Waldo almost winked as he said it, and it came crashing in on me that he'd left Ogo on Skarr deliberately. Leaving him stuck behind the barrier forever was part of his plan to destroy Ogo's father, the King, and take over Logra. No wonder Lucella had warned us that Waldo mustn't find out that Ogo was here. Ogo was the rightful heir. Waldo would kill him rather than give him back Logra or all that treasure of his.

Waldo did his disgusting sigh again. "Such a headstrong little boy! He gave me the slip at the very moment the Chaldeans rejected my pleas for peace, and I lost him. I was forced to put up the barrier and leave him." He shrugged sadly. "What else could I do?"

"You're the wizard," I said. "Was a simple search spell beyond your talent? It would have found him in a trice." It made Ogo smile a little, which pleased me. He was looking so grim.

Waldo shook his head at me sorrowfully. "Dear me, Aileen! You're beginning to sound like your Aunt Beck. All snap."

"Good!" I said. But the thought of Aunt Beck took the heart out of me. She would have known far better than I did how to deal with this man. I daren't ask what he'd done with her and the others for fear of his reply. He smiled. I hated the way he smiled, as if he were tasting you. I was too frightened by him to think straight, and I forced myself to calm down. I thought about the scent of the sea I'd smelled and the seaweed wrapping the calf, and a horrible idea came to me. "How did you make the barrier?" I asked. "It would need massive power. Did you do it with the winged bull's power?"

Waldo clapped his hands. "Clever Aileen!" he pretended to applaud me. "That's exactly what I did.

He agreed to *become* the barrier, which of course made it impenetrable. What's more, he agreed to *remain* the barrier until I sent him word that the war was over and Logra was safe from the attacks of the Chaldeans and their Guardians. We imagined it would be for a week or so, but time ran on. Life was good. The people were on my side. Somehow or other they'd got the idea that the Chaldeans had taken our little Prince Hugo hostage and then put the barrier in place." He shrugged and his gold necklaces jingled. "Why change things?"

My heart ached for the poor bull. I imagined him buried under mountains of water, holding the great wall in place, a prisoner of his own agreement with Waldo.

Waldo slapped the calf's flank, and it flinched. "It seems to have taken it out of the old fellow, doesn't it?" His round face suddenly flushed with anger. "He would have stayed as the barrier too, if it hadn't been for the other three Guardians interfering. They couldn't prevent the barrier. The Guardians couldn't use their power directly against another Guardian, but the three of them could insert that proviso that it would come down if a Wise Woman and a man from each island crossed it. I was annoyed at the time, but it's turned out rather well. Now you're here, I can get rid of all you troublemakers in one fell swoop."

As he talked, boasting and sucking, I found that if I half closed my eyes, I could see he was soaking up power. I could see it flowing out of the calf, like blood, and into Waldo. And the calf was dwindling. It really was smaller than it had been when I first saw it, as if he were eating the little creature alive. Waldo was using the greatest magic in our world to defeat us. There is nothing greater than the power of a Guardian. I was ready to cry.

Ogo asked about the tunnel in the air that had kidnapped Alasdair and my father. But Waldo was ready to leave now and stood up. His purple robes couldn't disguise his squat flabbiness once he was on his feet, though they had quite concealed the silly-looking throne he'd been perched on, piled high with cushions to raise him up. "We knew there was a special magic in Skarr," he said briskly.

"Aunt Beck," I agreed.

He flicked a look at me—almost as if he felt sorry for me. "And others," he said vaguely. "We had to prevent them concocting some form of retaliation to the barrier. To do that, we needed as priceless a hostage as Skarr had in our beloved Prince Hugo." He treated Ogo to a sneery little smile, and my heart sank. The smile made it quite clear he knew exactly who Ogo was. "It took a lot of work, but between us, Mevenne and I did a good job on that tunnel."

I wasn't surprised that Mevenne was in on it. It all fitted. Ogo wasn't surprised either. He was looking even grimmer. "I suppose she helped kidnap Alasdair because she wanted her son Donal to take over as High King of the Chaldeans after Farlane dies?"

Waldo was suddenly on the other side of the great room. "Or before," he said. "And sacrificing that other idiot son of theirs, Ivar, made his mother and father appear staunchly loyal to the cause of the Chaldeans. Above suspicion. I insisted on that in return for my making Donal High King. But of course, the real ruler of all the Chaldeans will be myself." He fingered the gold bands round his neck. "I'll have such fun."

From the look on his cruel-eyed face, I knew Waldo had it in mind to kill us now. "Forgive me, my dears," he said. "I've some executions to attend to. Public ones." He beckoned as if he were inviting us to come with him. But he wasn't. A door-size lump of the rocky wall rolled obediently toward him. He stepped through the hole it had left and closed it behind him.

"Quick!" I shouted. But Ogo was already pounding up the steps we had come in by.

He was back in a minute. "He's closed the fish's mouth," he told me. "We can't get out."

I sat down on the silly throne because my legs were shaking too much to stand up anymore. We were trapped and had been left to die. Ogo said confidently, "Beck will find us, and your father; there's a mass of magic among them all. They'll come." His face went the grimmest yet when I explained that they couldn't free themselves, or us. The huge power the calf was giving Waldo would easily swamp theirs. They would be executed without ever knowing what had happened to us.

Ogo tried to untie the calf then, but none of the ties holding it would come apart, even when he hacked at them with his sword. The poor creature was trussed up in its own strength. Only Waldo could free it, and he never would.

"At least he hasn't left us sitting in the dark," I said, trying to look cheerful. "And I'm sure we'll work something out." It didn't sound convincing. How could it? I hadn't an idea in my head what it could be.

Ogo gave me a polite little smile, so I knew he'd guessed I hadn't. He came and sat next to me on the floor, being careful not to bend Green Greet's four feathers in his sword belt, and said comfortingly, "I know you will."

I thought about Green Greet's sort of signposts that

had led us here. "Surely Green Greet didn't bring us down here to be buried alive," I said. "And *why* is there still light? Waldo wouldn't do us any favors. Someone else must be making the light for us."

"What are you looking at?" Ogo's question seemed to come from far off. I was watching the stream of power running across the ground from the shivering calf and through the rock where Waldo had left. If I looked at it really hard, with half-closed eyes, tiny, shimmering fragments rose from it and broke into tinier flakes of light that floated in the dark and lit the room. "It's the calf," I said. "He's giving us light. Even though he's drained of power, he's helping us."

Ogo jumped up excitedly. "Oh, *now* I see," he said. "Waldo gave himself away when he said the Guardians couldn't use their power directly against another Guardian. That means the other Guardians can't work against him to free the winged bull because Waldo is full of its Guardian power, but they are doing everything they can to help *you* do it."

"Me!" I shrieked. "How can I—"

"Oh, don't start all that 'I'm a talentless midget' stuff." He was really cross. "Didn't Waldo say there was special magic in Skarr? He meant you. And didn't the Lady say you were outstanding? And think how pleased Plug-Ugly was to see you when we turned up on the Lone Land." He folded his arms and stood in front of me. "Get on with it," he said firmly, "before Waldo kills everyone. I'll do whatever you want to help."

I think I felt the stupidest I ever had. To fill in time, I went and put my feet against the stream of power and watched it well up over my shoes like thick liquid or the finest silk ever made. I could hear it, too. It made a faint thrumming sound like a swarm of honeybees or distant thunder. It reminded me of the Wise Woman's hymn: "I am the thunder of the bull that gores." And that led me on to think about other bits of the hymn. Ogo says I stood and thought for minutes on end. My mind was jumping from one bit of the hymn to another: "I am the salmon leaping the fall. . . . I am the note of the bird. Verily the cunning of the cat is in me. . . . The fire is in me that gives the dragon wings, and this I will use when the purpose merits."

I knelt beside the calf and lifted the strands of seaweed from his soaking back. "Golden One," I said, "Lord of the East, let's reclaim your magic. I am not a Guardian but, somewhere in me, I have the power. Help me if you can."

At first it didn't work at all, and I almost allowed myself to believe that it never would. Ogo kept saying, "Keep going. Keep going. What are you doing?"

It was impossibly difficult to concentrate and to explain at the same time that I was trying to reverse the flow of the power and draw it back from Waldo and into the calf. It sounded a little too fanciful to be likely as well. I went on hauling in my mind's eye, but the power just stretched like good dough or else it ran away through my fingers. Instead of explaining, I asked, "Did you know you were the King's son and heir to the throne of Logra?"

"To begin with, yes. But after a while I decided it was a story I'd made up to comfort myself for everyone calling me the Ogre of Logra. I still wished it was true, though. One of the castle children told me that the castle well was a wishing well and that if you wished at full moon—"

"Bless you, Ogo," I interrupted. "That's the way to do it!"

"My pleasure. Do what?"

I made a great winch in my mind—the sort that holds the rope that lowers and raises the bucket in a well—and I put it into the stream of power. It wrapped greedily round the winch just as Waldo would. I caught it, twisted it round to secure it, then turned a handle, as if I were drawing a pail of well water. It resisted, but I went on turning. It felt as heavy as a bucket of stones, but I turned and turned until sweat poured off me.

I heard Ogo whisper my name. He was pointing at the calf. He had stopped shivering, and the tangle of dark magic holding him down was shriveling up like burning wool. Suddenly he struggled onto his front, gathered his hooves underneath him and, with a pushing effort, stood up on shaky legs. I went on turning the power faster and harder, and a small sprocket of golden curls appeared on the calf's forehead; then two nubbins of ebony black horns pushed up between his ears. He swung his head slowly to look at me with such a passion for living that it made me smile, and I worked harder. The small wings straightened, and their color deepened to cerulean—not feathers, not scales, but somehow both. I turned and turned my mind's eye handle, and the calf grew.

He had grown to twice the size when the power snapped to an end. The handle was whipped from my hand as it unwound back into the calf, whirling faster and faster, and he grew and grew.

Ogo pulled me to my feet and clapped me on the back. I couldn't stop smiling, I was so pleased. We were almost dancing with our success when I noticed the water spreading across the floor toward us from the steps we'd come down. As we looked, it began to pour in. The fountain must have been blocked off when Waldo closed the fish's mouth. The water had nowhere else to go except down the steps and in here. It was rushing in now. We would be drowned.

I was so angry that all our work and effort would come to nothing that I felt a power in me that nearly burst my ribs. I rushed at the wall where Waldo had gone and yelled at it to move aside. And it did. I was so astonished that I sat down on the ground with a splash and Ogo had to shout at me to go. I thought he was coming with me, but when I turned back for him in the gap in the wall, he was still standing by the bull, who had grown level with his chest by now. He called, "I'm staying here with Logra's Guardian. We'll look after each other." The water was already over his shoes, but he grinned and waved me on. "Besides, it's not exactly our sort of door you've made, Aileen."

I could hardly bear to leave them behind. If it hadn't been for my anger driving me on, I might not have. I saw what he meant about the door I'd made, though, when I went through the gap and walked smack into earth. It was cold but kind, and it yielded as I pulled myself up through it. It was like climbing a crumbly ladder. Then my head hit a ceiling. My anger moved it apart with a crash. I realized it was a floor, not a ceiling, when I stepped up into a dark bedchamber with nothing much there but a four-poster bed. A thin, mild-looking man, wrapped in shawls, was propped up in it on pillows. He stared at me in surprise from where he was trying to read by the light of a miserable lamp.

"Excuse me," I panted. It was all I could think of saying as he peered at me in the half-light. I must have looked a fine sight with my wet dress covered in earth and my hair wild and muddy.

"That's the way my brother Waldo usually arrives," he said. "But you're definitely not him. Who are you?"

"Oh! You're the King?" I gasped.

"I *was* King," he answered me gently. "But I'm too ill now."

"No, you're not," I snapped. Perhaps I really was getting like Aunt Beck. "You just think you are. Let's have a proper look at you." I ran over to the windows and pushed back the shutters, one after the other.

"Please don't," he cried. "Waldo says the light will kill me."

"He's lying," I retorted, and threw back the last shutter. He blinked a little in the light that flooded in. "See," I panted. "Sunlight! And you're still as lively as a flea. But look at the state of you! You're weighed down with sick magic." I rushed at the four-poster bed's canopy, and I clawed at it. It was laden with spells that were hanging over him in brown, lumpy strings, like dirty, badly spun wool.

"What a very vigorous person you are," he said as it crashed down round his bed.

"Sorry," I said. "It only came over me today—the vigor, I mean—and I'm not sure of my own strength yet."

He smiled a little. "It seems substantial."

I could only hope it was going to be substantial enough. "Get up, Your Majesty," I commanded, and he stood up on his bed in a wobbly sort of way. "Jump over the canopy."

"Jump?" he asked, with a doubtful look at it over the edge of his bed.

"Oh! Come on," I said encouragingly, and took him by the elbow. I shouldn't have done that. He leaped nimbly enough over the vile magic, but it rose up and hit my right arm in a hissing burn that made my flesh smoke. Even without the bull's power, Waldo was a wizard to reckon with. I spoke Rees's quenching spell, and the burning went out in a stinging steam. My anger doubled.

The King was offering me one of his shawls to bandage my arm, but there was no time. "Where do public executions get done?" I asked urgently.

"They don't anymore, but they used to take place in the entrance courtyard."

I raced to the door, then hesitated, picturing Ogo

up to his middle in water, by now. His father seemed so sad and broken that I took a risk and raised his hopes. "Hugo's here," I told him. His face lit up, and I ran.

I could tell I was running in huge zigzags, which made me feel a bit dizzy and rather daft too, until I realized there was sense to it. I was avoiding the crowds of people thronging down the staircases to watch the executions in the courtyard. So I was still in time.

It was a horrible sight when I got there. They were all lined up with their hands tied behind them: Aunt Beck, Ivar, and Prince Alasdair, Rees, Ogo's nurse, Lucella, and all the rest. Poor Finn was crying for the loss of Green Greet, who was nowhere to be seen. My father and Riannan were both gagged. I supposed it was in case they sang an enchantment on the black-hooded executioner. He was standing, with his ax, on a dais in the center of the courtyard, next to the execution block. Two soldiers were just putting some wooden steps in place for the prisoners to mount. Ranks of yet more soldiers stood round them. At the far end, there was a higher dais, where Waldo was sitting with several prosperous-looking men and their gaudy wives. The rich, grain-hoarding merchants, I imagined. Directly beneath them was a flock of wizards in their purple robes, and in front of them, the empty-headed ministers sitting on chairs. I could see them properly now, thanks to my vigor, as the King called it, and I realized that there was magic, like matted wool, on top of their heads, squashing the wits out of them.

I hid behind a fat pillar in the palace doorway and wondered what to do. There was so little time. The gates were already closing on the last of the raggedy crowds of spectators, spilling in to stand where they could for the best view. "Death to the spies," some of them were chanting. Waldo's expression was the single thing that gave me hope: he looked uneasy. The sucking feeling coming from him was still strong but unchanneled. I ducked as it moved fast toward me and went sluggishly over my head. Waldo must have realized that he'd lost his hold on the winged bull, and the sucking was searching around for another source of power. Well, you're not having mine, I thought fiercely. I've only just found it, and I need every grain of it. Waldo was looking downright alarmed now and clearly wanted to get the killing done with. He raised his hand, and the soldiers began dragging Ivar toward the steps up to the executioner.

I need an army, I thought in despair. Nothing but an army could stop this now. I need an army. The thought thundered in my head, and I heard my voice boom, "I need an army!" Everyone looked round for the culprit; some even spotted my pillar and started toward me. A great rap on the courtyard gates stopped them in their tracks, and the gates were flung open from the outside. Bless me! I thought. I may not be able to move people the way Aunt Beck can, but I can move stone.

In marched my army—all the statues from the Royal Avenue. Clumping and crunching, they heaved into the yard: kings, wizards, queens, and gods. There were even the sort that were just noble heads on plinths, who came hopping in on the stumps of their columns. They all laid about them, whamming and whacking with stone arms and scepters and wands and thunderbolts. Soldiers were going down like skittles, and the squalling crowd was running this way and that to keep out of my army's reach. The silly ministers crouched behind their chairs and got thwacked sensible. The purple wizards, who were frantically trying to construct an iron curtain between my army and themselves, kept being walloped off course. I saw Waldo use his waning power to wrap himself in stone so that he looked like one of the statues.

We would have won, but then something appeared in the air. At first, it bounced and wove about like the end of a leather pipe when water is gushing through it and the water flows first one way, then switches away to spout in another direction. Then it steadied and widened and became a hole in the air that was big enough for Mevenne to step out of, onto Waldo's dais. Donal followed, gorgeous in gold bangles, and then his father, King Kenig.

"Mother!" Ivar screamed. "Help me."

And Mevenne, swirling in her dark aura, laughed and stretched out her hand. Statues began to splinter and crack and fall. They groaned as they came apart. Mevenne even mistook Waldo for one of them. He emerged squatly from a cloud of his own rubble, looking bruised and furious. Some of the people were cheering, as she smashed my army to pieces. Then Donal pointed at Ivar and said something to Mevenne, who nodded. Poor Ivar was completely stunned. Aunt Beck had kept it from him that his mother had tried to kill him once already, but it was plain that's what she intended to do now and he was terrified of her. Even so, he was the bravest I've ever seen him. As Mevenne stretched out her hand toward him, he turned to Riannan and tried to smile.

"No!" I cried. "Don't kill him."

And the yard filled with bloodred—bloodred coils of scales and talons and flame. Sheets of flame shot across the space and folded Mevenne in blindingly white heat, and she sort of evaporated. Kenig and Donal, too. A single gold bangle rolled, like a little hoop, along the charred dais where they'd been standing.

I saw Waldo seize a piece of the flame. Don't let him, Blodred, I thought, because I knew the flame was her. Don't let him use your power against you. But Waldo didn't have time. The crowd was screaming and running. The executioner was thrown from the platform. The yard was crisscrossed with cracks. I saw Aunt Beck move the entire line of prisoners away from the center. I had time to think—Oh! *That's* how she does it—before chunks of stone and paving were hurled into the air and a truly glorious golden bull rose out of the ground on blue wings. Ogo was riding on his back, every bit a prince. He said later he didn't know how his skull wasn't cracked. The ground closed smoothly under them, and Ogo leaped off and rushed to free the prisoners. Waldo tried to run. He was like a floppy sponge, running on the spot, flailing the air as Green Greet came screeching in above his head to stop him. The bull lowered his head and charged. I saw him roll Waldo up in the bellowing rage of his horns, and Waldo was over and done.

The air above the courtyard was filled now with the bull's gold and blue, and with the red of Blodred and the green of Green Greet. I looked and looked but I couldn't see Plug-Ugly, and my heart nearly stopped with fear for him. Then I felt the pressure of his head against the back of my hand, and the cool of his nose that came, like a good-bye, before he was up there too: the gray stripes and splotches of the Beast of the North. They were themselves as we knew them, but, at the same time, they were mightier versions of themselves. They darkened the courtyard with their great shapes as they danced and wove above us, then moved together with one deafening roar of joy. Long after they had gone, we could hear the sound of that cry flying and fading northward and east and away to the south and west. Then there was complete quiet.

My father and Riannan began to sing. I don't

remember what, but I remember the peace it brought to everyone there. I don't really remember much more in detail. I remember everyone hugging one another, and the King hurrying out of the palace in his dressing gown to the cheers of the crowd, and the humble way Ogo went down on one knee to him, and I remember the glow inside me when Aunt Beck said she was proud enough of me to burst. The statues pieced themselves together—robes, bodices and earlobes, chips and splinters reassembled—and they trundled away. One or two cast wistful looks back, as if they'd have liked to join in the celebrations that were starting and that lasted for days. I remember hugging Ogo and him hugging me, and him saying, "Isn't it a coincidence, Aileen? We Logran kings have the same custom as the Wise Women of Skarr."

"Indeed," I said, knowing by the grin he was wearing from ear to ear that he was lying.

"Oh, yes," he lied. "You Wise Women aren't the only ones. Just as you choose a husband early on"—he smiled at me—"we kings can choose a queen, too."

"Is that a fact?" I said, smiling back, wide enough to split my face with happiness. I remember Finn coming up, with tears in his beard, and saying it certainly was a fact, and my father laughing. He kissed the top of my head, which made me feel like a crowned queen already, and said that yes, it most definitely was a fact.

And I remember, as I'm writing this, walking over the moor, weeks later, in the first of the early Skarr frosts. The moon was rising, and I was hurrying through the dusk on my way to collect my things. Beck and I were to move to Dromray to join Prince Alasdair and his father, the High King Farlane. What a reunion that had been! My father and Lucella were already there. Ogo was to come later and train to be a king, though I didn't think he was in need of much training. As I passed the Place, I stopped dead. From where I was standing, I could just see my cousin Kenig's castle down on the foreshore. It was Ivar's now, and empty, because he was at the Pandy with Riannan. But in my vision that I'd had during my initiation, the castle hadn't been there at all. I believe my vision had been telling me that its ugly magic would soon be wiped out forever.

Much later, I knew that our croft had appeared dark because I was to be the Wise Woman not just of Skarr but of all the islands of Chaldea—and of Logra too, when Ogo and I were crowned. We islanders would share our wisdom from now on.

And when all that had come into being, I sometimes get the urge on me to take a little sailing boat out on my own. I sail and search in my mind's eye until I find the Land of Lone. I come ashore, climb the small cliff, cross the space of scuttling, speeding little creatures, and walk through the ruined temple. I hear his cry from above me, and the Lone Cat, the ugliest cat I ever beheld, bounds gladly from pillar to pillar toward me. We stay awhile with each other, then part.

Dear Readers,

When I first read this lovely, searching, last novel by my sister, Diana Wynne Jones, it stopped short where she became too ill to continue. It was a shock: it was like being woken from sleepwalking or nearly running off the edge of a cliff. It had elements of a much happier time in our childhood, too.

Diana wrote her first full-length novel when she was fourteen years old. It filled a series of exercise books, and she would read the newest section to us, her two younger sisters, in bed at night. When she suddenly stopped reading, we would wail, "Go on, go on. What happens next?" and she'd say, "Don't you understand? I haven't written any more yet." And we would go to sleep, agog for the next section. It always duly turned up the next night, which is where the present day diverged so unhappily from our childhood past. This time, the next section couldn't turn up. Her book had ended without an ending. Diana Wynne Jones was such a masterly storyteller that it was impossible to imagine where she planned to take it. She left no notes: she never ever made any. Her books always came straight out of her extraordinary mind onto the page, and she never discussed her work while it was in progress. There was not so much as a hint of what she was up to, and it seemed *The Islands of Chaldea* was lost to its readers.

Then the family suggested that I might complete it. I was nervous. Diana was my big sister, and big sisters notoriously don't like kid sisters messing with their stuff. Particularly when the big sister in question is very good at her stuff. Nevertheless, her family and friends had a meeting to pool their ideas on how the story might continue. We were all steeped in her work. We'd all known her well. Everyone was sure that, by the end of the afternoon, we would come up with something. We didn't; she had us all stumped. Eventually, Diana's son closed the session with, "Well, Ursula, you'll just have to make it up."

It took months. I scoured the text for those clues that Diana always dropped for her readers as to where the narrative was headed, and which I'd always unfailingly overlooked until I'd read the final page. I hadn't changed. I found nothing.

Initially, I was working at the National Theatre in London, too (I'm an actress when I'm wearing my other hat), and the play I was in was full of eerie happenings and second sight. I would catch the bus home across the river after the show and dream weird and often frightening dreams as I tried to break into my sister's thinking. I believe I got even closer to her at this point than I was during her lifetime. But although I hunted and pondered, nothing came to me. Then, just as I was beginning to feel like a sous chef, endlessly producing flat soufflés under the slightly disapproving gaze of the Chef, I found one of her clues. I found it near the beginning of her manuscript. And we were off!

When I started to write, it came easily. It was almost as if Diana were at my elbow, prompting, prodding, turning sentences around, working alongside—and then it was finished, and she was gone again. That was a terrible wrench. But her book was there — complete.

So far, no one who has come to *The Islands of Chaldea* freshly has spotted exactly where Diana Wynne Jones left off and I begin. Perhaps you will be able to, perhaps you won't. It doesn't really matter. It is intrinsically and utterly her book, and I hope you and all its readers love it as much as I do.

Sincerely,

Ursula Jones
Itzac, November 2013